T0286396

THE BOOK OF REYKJAVIK

The Book of Reykjavik

EDITED BY VERA JÚLÍUSDÓTTIR
& BECCA PARKINSON

Part of Comma's 'Reading the City' series

First published in Great Britain by Comma Press, 2021.

www.commapress.co.uk

'The Dead are Here with Us at Christmas' was first published in *Afleiðingar* by
Draumsýn (2017). 'Two Foxes' was first published in *Smáglæpir* by Sæmundur (2017).
'Island' was first published in *Takk fyrir að láta mig vita* by Benedikt (2016). 'Without
You, I'm Half' was first published in *Doris deyr* by JPV (2010). 'The Gardeners' was
first published in *Leitin að dýragarðinum* by Almenna bókafélagið (1988). 'Incursion' was
first published in *Ó fyrir framan* by Vaka-Helgafell (1992). 'Keep Sleeping, My Love' was
first published in *Sofðu ást mín* by Mál og menning (2016). 'Home' was first published
in *Kláði* by Partus (2018). 'When His Eyes are on You, You're the Virgin Mary' was first
published in *Á meðan hann horfir á þig ertu María mey* by Bjartur (1998).

A CIP catalogue record of this book is available from the British Library.

ISBN: 191097403X
ISBN-13: 978-1-91097-403-2

This book has been translated with financial support from the
Icelandic Literature Center.

 ICELANDIC LITERATURE CENTER

The publisher gratefully acknowledges the support of Arts Council England.

Contents

FOREWORD   vii
Sjón

INTRODUCTION   xiii
Vera Júlíusdóttir

ISLAND   I
Friðgeir Einarsson
Translated by Larissa Kyzer

THE GARDENERS   II
Einar Már Guðmundsson
Translated by Victoria Cribb

KEEP SLEEPING, MY LOVE   29
Andri Snær Magnason
Translated by Lytton Smith

HOME   43
Fríða Ísberg
Translated by Larissa Kyzer

TWO FOXES   49
Björn Halldórsson
Translated by Larissa Kyzer

WITHOUT YOU, I'M HALF   59
Kristín Eiríksdóttir
Translated by Larissa Kyzer

CONTENTS

REYKJAVIK NIGHTS   71
Auður Jónsdóttir
Translated by Meg Matich

INCURSION   79
Þórarinn Eldjárn
Translated by Philip Roughton

WHEN HIS EYES ARE ON YOU, YOU'RE THE VIRGIN MARY   83
Guðrún Eva Mínervudóttir
Translated by Meg Matich

THE DEAD ARE HERE WITH US AT CHRISTMAS   89
Ágúst Borgþór Sverrisson
Translated by Lytton Smith

ABOUT THE CONTRIBUTORS   95

Foreword

Reykjavik – Gomorrah

As a kid born in Reykjavik in 1962, I was, from an early age, aware that even though we had access to luxuries such as seven cinemas, three theatres, a high street, hotdog stands and taxis, it was all overshadowed, in the national imagination, by the simpler, purer life enjoyed in the smaller fishing towns, even more so the rural areas where people still trod the same ground as the heroes of the Sagas while enveloped by landscapes made sublime in the poems of Iceland's nineteenth-century Romantic poets. I had this impression confirmed every summer when I went to stay with relatives in the East Fjords. There, I was taught many a verse about the misery of Reykjavik, and when it was time for me to return to Sin City in the autumn, I was sent off with blessings heaped upon me, particularly by the older people. The next summer my return would be celebrated as if I had escaped from the mouth of the Leviathan. That is to say, the book you hold in your hands contains stories from the most despised place in Iceland, the tiny nations' only city and capital, Reykjavik.

Over the past three centuries, as it grew from village to town to city, the small human habitat of 'Smokey Bay' (as its old Norse name means) has served as a subject of ridicule and contempt by Icelanders and foreigners alike. Not least by its own inhabitants, most of whom had moved there from the beautiful countryside or remote, wholesome villages. Its streets and its people were dirty and lazy, it harboured every possible carnal vice and corruption of the mind, it was simultaneously uncultured and snobbish, and as proof of its degradation, it had the only purpose-built prison on the island. Not even its prominent role in the early history of the country, as the place of residence of Iceland's first settler, Ingólfur Arnarson, gave it any credit in the eyes of those who believed they saw it for what it really was: a Gomorrah of the North.

All of these negative feelings might have been influenced by the fact that the unpopular Danish government chose to place its officials and offices there, in the centuries when we were one of their colonies. But as the focus of this spite has always been on the bad habits of the degenerate *Reykvíkingar* (Reykja-vikings) themselves, it seems the blame belongs to the locus itself and the locals, whose only excuse was that they might be considered the victims of an evil, overbearing 'locus genii'.

The picture given of it by the English priest and scholar Sabine Baring-Gould, who visited Iceland in the summer of 1862, and who like all visitors was forced to suffer a few nights in the wretched town, sums it up nicely:

> Reykjavik is a jumble of wooden shanties, pitched down wherever the builder listed. Some of the houses are painted white, the majority black, one has broken out in green shutters, another is daubed over with orange. [...] The moment that the main thoroughfares are quitted, the stench emitted from the smaller houses becomes insupportable. Decayed fish, offal, filth of every description, is tossed anywhere for the rain to wash away, or for the passer-by to trample into the ground. The fuel made use of is dry seaweed, fishbones,

and any refuse which can be coaxed to smoulder or puffed into a blaze; so that the smoke, as may well be imagined, is anything but grateful to the olfactory nerves. [...] Now let us push down the street, avoiding the drunken man who lies wallowing on the ground, sobbing as though his heart would break, because his equally drunken adversary will not turn his back and stand steady, to let him have a comfortable kick.

And for a long while, the only stories told about Reykjavik were the ones printed in travelogues of foreigners like Baring-Gould, who came to the country in search of a hyperborean Arcadia untarnished by the modern age, only to be bitterly disappointed.

It wasn't until the late nineteenth century that we start seeing works of local literature, successfully chronicling the lives of the people who actually lived there.

Unfortunately, it didn't particularly help the city's poor image, as the father of the Reykjavik story, Gestur Pálsson, was also a disciple of the Naturalist school and its mission to expose social ills. He burst onto the scene in 1890, by giving a public lecture about the sorry state of the town, and then proceeded to establish his view in short stories about its downtrodden and invisible poor. Next in line was Þórbergur Þórðarson who published a book of Chaplinesque episodes about his struggle in the '20s to live the life of a man of the mind while being stuck in a cesspool, literally starving while his fellow citizens looked on with indifference.

And then, between 1931 and 1938, Þórunn Elfa Magnúsdóttir published her three-volume novel *Daughters of Reykjavik (Dætur Reykjavikur)* describing young women trying to find their place in life in the somewhat hostile, somewhat exciting city of 28,000 inhabitants. The title itself was a challenge to the negative stereotype. It had an air of gaiety to it and it claimed that Reykjavik had come into its own as a setting for stories and as a place one could belong to. The same year that Magnúsdóttir published the first volume of her novel saw the publication of the poetry collection *It's a Beautiful World* (*Fagra Veröld*) by Tómas Guðmundsson. In its vignettes, we see the first attempt at finding beauty in the fledgling city. The young people of Reykjavik welcomed it, but its lyrical celebration of traffic lights and secret rendezvous in back streets, fell on deaf ears in the rest of the country. And then, as the village expanded into a town, and that town became a city, the stories multiplied.

The traumatic events of the Spanish influenza in November of 1918 was our baptism into modernity, the invasion of the British Army in 1940 was our confirmation day (followed by a night where we had our first smoke, drink and sexual experience), the Fisher-Spassky World Chess Championship in 1972 signalled our engagement to the wider world, the Reagan-Gorbatchev summit of 1986 was our marriage to it, and ever since then we've been the unfaithful partner in that relationship.

One of the milestones of twentieth-century Icelandic literature is the short story collection *From Sunday night to Monday* (*Sunnudagskvöld til mánudagsmorguns*) by Ásta Sigurðardóttir. Published in 1961, it is written with restrained anger and compassion for those the author had broken bread with on her own turbulent journey through the dark underbelly of Reykjavik. It was a journey cut short in 1971 when Sigurðardóttir died from alcoholism at the age of forty-one. Today, her slim book is seen as a modernist, feminist classic, and it is the unavoidable starting point for anyone who wishes to tell stories from the misshapen urban cluster at the farthest edge of Europe that was her home. By avoiding the epic tale, otherwise so beloved by the Icelanders, I believe she proposed that it is only in the small forms of literature, the fragmented narratives, we can begin to understand Reykjavik.

So, it is fitting that the reader of this volume is transported to this most miserable of places, through short stories by some of its finest authors.

Abandon all hope. Welcome to the City of Fear.

Sjón,
Reykjavik, May 2021

Introduction

'Glöggt er gests augað' goes an old Icelandic saying, which might translate as, 'a guest has a keen eye'. A visitor to Reykjavik will notice things that the locals have long since stopped noticing. The serene beauty of the surrounding mountains; the Snæfellsjökull glacier floating above the horizon across the bay like a mirage; the ocean waves lapping at its shores; the hot tubs where the locals meet to discuss politics – our version of the forum in ancient Greece – the stories that can be found beneath every stone, in every back alley.

With just over 200,000 inhabitants in the Greater Reykjavik area, some would call Reykjavik a large town rather than a city. Growing up here in the eighties and nineties, I longed to live in a bigger place. And moving away in the late '90s and living in the US and UK for nearly two decades, I found, on my return, that Reykjavik had transformed itself. No longer just a remote spot on the map, it had become a destination in its own right.

Today, Reykjavik is a hip metropolis, complete with artisan coffee shops, designer clothing boutiques, and tourists from all over the world. New neighbourhoods have sprung up on the outskirts of the city and once sleepy suburbs have become multicultural hubs of activity. An award-winning concert hall has appeared next to what used to be a humble working harbour. Instead of cod and herring, Icelanders now export music, art and literature. Writers from Reykjavik have garnered international awards and received critical acclaim and recognition far beyond these shores, thanks to the work of excellent translators. For all intents and purposes, Reykjavik has come of age.

The city's designation, in 2011, as a UNESCO City of Literature – making it only the fifth city in the world to receive the honour – also gave the city a boost. The Vigdís International Centre for Multilingualism and Intercultural Understanding was opened at the University of Iceland in 2017, and annual events like the Reykjavik Book Fair, Reykjavik Reads and numerous other initiatives have also sprung up to promote literature and reading in the city.

That said, the people of Reykjavik have never needed much encouragement in this department. A good example of the central role literature plays in the life of its citizens is that every November, a catalogue of all books published in Iceland that year is delivered to every household in the country. For many people, an essential part of the build-up to Christmas is to browse through this catalogue and choose the books they will gift family and friends, as well as those to add to their own wish list. Almost every Icelander gets at least one book for Christmas. Another example is the statistic that as many as one in ten people in Iceland will at some point in their lives publish a book![1]

My mother was the head librarian of the public library in downtown Reykjavik and as a child, I would sit for hours among the ceiling-high bookshelves and lose track of time as I read my way through the children's section. I felt at home this great fortress of books, with its white-painted stone walls, imposing shelves and staircases, its reassuring smell of book dust and solid oak. Later I discovered that I hadn't been the only one. Many have sung the praises of this 'castle' in the heart of the old town, where their lifelong love of literature and writing was kindled as children. Among them are many of Reykjavik's best-known writers.

In recent years, as more and more people from all around the globe have visited Reykjavik as tourists, so the interest in the cultural output of this small but over-performing city has grown. Yet Icelandic society can seem close-knit and impenetrable to outsiders. Icelanders are not exactly known for being outgoing and have perhaps yet to quite master the art of small talk. With that in mind, it is interesting that so much artistic expression and creativity comes from this small place. Maybe it's *because* the people of Reykjavik do not wear their emotions on their sleeve that they have so much bottled up looking to be expressed through art and literature. To survive and thrive in a city like Reykjavik, a rich inner life is certainly a useful trait. Although I live and work in Reykjavik and am once again part of its close-knit community, I hope that I have not lost the ability to see it through a 'guest's eye'. When selecting the stories for *The Book of Reykjavik* I have tried to do so with both perspectives – that of the local and the guest – in mind.

Many of the stories in this anthology reflect the ever-present dialogue, even tension, between urbanity and the rugged landscape that surrounds Reykjavik. The sea, mountains and lava fields bleed into the cityscape and very much influence the culture of the place. This conflict between a not-so-distant rural past and new-fangled city life is a theme shared by the three of the stories here.

In 'Two Foxes' by Björn Halldórsson, a sleepless suburbanite who lives in a new neighbourhood built on a lava field after the economic crash comes face-to-face with an arctic fox in his backyard. This unexpected encounter brings back a childhood memory of coming across a fox during a family camping trip, and reminds the protagonist of the generational difference between his own reaction to the animal and his father's, who grew up on a farm.

'The Gardeners' by Einar Már Guðmundsson tells a comic tale of former farmers turned urban gardeners. Set in a time of rapid expansion for the city, due to mass internal migration from the countryside, it shows the newcomers struggling to adjust to life in a big town and trying to carve out new identities and careers for themselves, in spite of the past's insistence on 'cropping up' in the present.

In the more recently set 'Incursion' by Þórarinn Eldjárn, the owners of new luxury flats in downtown Reykjavik find an upsetting 'hidden defect' in their building in the form of strange, possibly supernatural sounds that. Every morning, they are awakened by what sounds like the ghostly echoes of the old carpentry workshop that once stood on that spot.

Other stories try to make sense of relationships in this unique mini-city. In 'Without You, I'm Half' by Kristín Eiríksdóttir, love appears permanently out of reach. The story culminates in a strange scene where an unknown voice on the phone professes her love. It is a love that takes after the ancient Platonic ideal of two halves that together form a whole.

In 'When His Eyes are on You, You're the Virgin Mary' by Guðrún Eva Mínervudóttir, a young woman who lives, and spends her free time in downtown Reykjavik – a 'downtown rat' according to the local lingo – flirts with disaster by engaging in unhealthy relationships with older, troubled men.

In 'Keep Sleeping, My Love' by Andri Snær Magnason, a man goes on a lonely nocturnal odyssey to the popular beauty spot Grótta to watch the sun set into the crater of the Snæfellsjökull glacier – a natural phenomenon that only occurs once a year. Every year since they first met, he and his girlfriend have visited Grótta to experience it together, until now, their relationship having grown tired and cold, along with the words they used to express their feelings for one another.

In 'Reykjavik Nights' by Auður Jónsdóttir, a recent divorcee is going through her second adolescence as she tries to find her feet after the breakdown of her relationship. Her tragicomic adventures in the Reykjavik nightlife scene are lovingly described, with a keen sense of the ridiculous.

'Home' by Fríða Ísberg shows a darker side of Reykjavik – this supposed paradise of gender equality. A young woman tries to make it safely home after a night out on the town. Every man she encounters in the street feels to her like a potential threat. Her vulnerability as a woman in this society is apparent in each careful step she takes towards the safety of home.

At the heart of the 'The Dead are Here with Us at Christmas' by Ágúst Borgþór Sverrisson lies the quiet drama about the way family bereavements and absences are felt most deeply in the holidays. A mother is determined to place a candle on her dead son's grave on Christmas Eve, even as her car breaks down and she has to seek help, to the deep annoyance and embarrassment of her sulking younger son who is driving with her.

'Island' by Friðgeir Einarsson explores a different kind of loss, told from the point of view of an ex-pat who returns to Reykjavik to attend his mother's funeral, only to realise that he has finally lost all social and emotional ties to his former home.

With *The Book of Reykjavik*, we hope to show the breadth and depth of Reykjavik's writing by including stories written by contemporary authors from different generations. We also kept an equal gender ratio, which is apt for a book dedicated to the capital of a country ranked as having the greatest gender equality in the world.

In a year in which a global pandemic forced us all into isolation, collecting these stories to be shared with the rest of the world felt especially important. Now, as the world starts to open up and visitors can be seen walking the streets of Reykjavik again, let us be grateful her stories can begin to be told, shared, and written once more.

Vera Júlíusdóttir,
Reykjavik, July 2021

Note

1. Rosie Goldsmith, 'Iceland: Where one in 10 people will publish a book', *BBC News*, 14 Oct 2013.

Island

Friðgeir Einarsson

Translated by Larissa Kyzer

I USUALLY LEAN BACK in my seat during landing, close my eyes and count backwards from 100 in threes: 100, 97, 94, and so on. It calms me. But this time, I felt like I needed to look out the window. Maybe because I'd been away so long, or out of a sense of duty. Maybe because I was in the window seat and not on the aisle like usual. There'd been a mix-up with the booking.

The plane descended and the rocky coastline came into view, as if it were rising up from the sea. Then I saw a spit of land stretching across the surface of the water, slowly but surely transforming into a country as I watched. Out at the furthest point, tucked in among sheer bluffs and nubbly crags, was a lightless lighthouse. Not far from there were a few houses in a grassy hollow, looking vulnerable and breakable from this distance. It was as if everything I was looking at was made of hastily cut-and-pasted paper and would fall to pieces at the slightest touch. That's how it looked from a distance, at least. And there's something appealing about this distance − the bird's eye view, so to speak. Isn't that what people like about mountain hikes and penthouse apartments? Not having to take part in all the goings-on below? Isn't that what people like about travelling by plane? An aeroplane is a distance-making machine.

A few years ago, I watched a live broadcast of a tsunami as it beat a path across some faraway country. The cameraman was up in a helicopter. At home in our living rooms, we viewers watched in silent terror as the wave took its time devouring buildings and streets, as cars, racing to stay ahead of it, vanished one by one into the tide and blended into a dark soup of earth and garbage. A trawler floated on the crest of the wave, and we're not talking about some dinghy here, we're talking a giant ship. You could easily imagine the astonishment and dread on the faces of the people below; it must have been terrifying. But from a distance, there was something calming about this destruction. From the air, the whole thing proceeded in silence.

That will be this country's fate, too, one day, I thought. In the end, the sea will wash those cottages away. Obliterate any sign that once, there were people here.

It didn't take long to organise the funeral. It would be held in a week. The old woman had seen to all the arrangements herself, chose the psalms and the coffin, and there was no question as to who would inherit what: I was the only beneficiary. By noon, everything seemed to be in order, and I took a taxi to my mother's apartment, which now belonged to me.

The taxi drove through a neighbourhood I knew well. I'd spent a lot of time here before I moved abroad, frequented coffeehouses and shops, joined the mingling masses on major holidays. I hadn't really expected that anything would have changed, but I still felt a sense of surprise – disappointment, almost – at just how much was basically the same as it was the last time I was here. There were some new signs here and there, and maybe more people out and about, but that was true everywhere.

The taxi driver was listening to some talk show on the radio, the kind where the host chats with people who call in about whatever is making headlines that day. When I got in, there was an elderly man on the line and, if I understood correctly (my Icelandic's a bit rusty), he was fixated on something some woman had said publicly about some international association or alliance. The host agreed and they started talking about the economy or something in that vein, which involved astronomically high figures.

The driver heaved a sigh and said something about border controls and people who worked in offices in mainland Europe. I told him that I was, effectively, a foreigner, and didn't understand the issue well enough to comment. He didn't say anything after that, and we continued listening to the radio without comment.

The old woman's apartment was pretty tidy. She'd lived in a nursing home for the past few years, and the apartment had, for the most part, stood vacant. There was nothing in the fridge, but there was a jar of instant coffee and an electric kettle on the counter, so I made myself a cup. Then I dusted the shelves and ran a damp cloth over the floor.

When that was done, there wasn't really anything left for me to do. And this was only the first day. I wouldn't be leaving for another week, give or take. There were hundreds of books in the apartment, most of them with pictures of old folks on the cover, but I didn't feel like reading. I hadn't read a word of Icelandic in years, maybe even a decade, on top of which, I had no interest in any of the contents.

Eventually, I'd have to price all this old junk or find some other way to get rid of it – the books, the bookcases they were stacked in, the whole lot of it.

I thought about going for a walk around the neighbourhood, but after thinking about it for a moment, I realised I didn't have the slightest interest in doing so. You always want to check out your surroundings when you arrive in a new place – or yes, a place you haven't been in a very long time. But the broad strokes remain the same no matter where you go. There's never anything new to see. Wherever you go, there are tarmacked streets and concrete pavements. The grocery stores sell the same things: milk, meat, bread, canned goods, coffee, fizzy drinks and sweets. If it's a small shop, they usually have more dry goods at higher prices. Other shops sell knickknacks, sunglasses, mass-produced toys and plastic whatnots, clothes that are basically the same no matter what country you're in – setting aside, of course, national costumes, although those are really only ever worn on festive occasions and at dance performances put on for tourists.

Most cities have some conspicuous landmark that people want to take pictures of. These are generally made of concrete, but sometimes bronze or other metals. In rural areas, people take pictures of the natural phenomena and strange locals. In poor areas, there are gravel roads and run-down houses – sometimes, they aren't even painted. Some places have animals that are novel for tourists, but you can usually see them in zoos, too. Hotel rooms always have a bed, a toilet, and a chair to sit in, otherwise people wouldn't want to sleep there. Sometimes, there's a TV. Watching TV in a foreign country can be interesting, but only for half a day or so. Sunsets can be impressive, particularly in places where there's lots of particulate matter in the air.

All of this – or stuff like this – is stuff I've seen many times on my travels. It's been a long time since I believed that anything could ever surprise me.

There was no TV in my mother's apartment. No doubt it was sent up to the nursing home so she could watch it there.

I wandered around the apartment, pausing for a moment in the doorway of the bedroom that had once been 'mine'. There was some rubbish in there that probably should have reminded me of something – objects connected to stuff I'd once been interested in and pictures of me when I was younger.

In my old closet, I found some of my old clothes – white jeans, a creamy yellow t-shirt, a mint-green tracksuit top made out of some sort of synthetic fabric and a pair of swimming trunks. The trunks used to be red but had faded to pink over the years.

There was a time when I enjoyed going to the pool, sitting in the hot pots. It's nice to bob around in warm water.

I changed clothes, folded the trousers I'd arrived in and hung up my shirt. I rolled up the swim trunks in a towel I found in the bathroom and put them in a plastic bag. It was mild out and even though I'd grown accustomed to much warmer weather, I decided to go on foot.

It felt weird walking around in my old clothes – like being someone else, if still someone I'd tried to be before. Not that it really made any difference. Everyone around here had long since forgotten me, irrespective of whether I was wearing old clothes or new.

It was a weekday, so there weren't a lot of people at the pool. The young woman at the front desk was wearing a light-coloured shirt that showed off how tanned she was. I nodded at her and snuck a peek at her nipples, which were visible under her t-shirt before taking off my sunglasses. It's just a thing I do, a sort of proclivity, you might say.

She asked if I was a senior citizen.

'There's a discount for seniors,' she explained in English.

'No, I'm not a senior citizen,' I answered.

'Sorry,' she said. 'I'm really bad at guessing people's ages.'

'It's alright,' I said, handing her my credit card. She ran it through the scanner. There was some sort of problem with the system and the transaction was a long time processing. She smiled, or at least quirked up one side of her mouth, and I tried to smile back. Then the payment went through and the machine spat out a white receipt with a barcode on it. She handed me the receipt and a stretchy, yellow rubber bracelet and explained that I should hold it up to a sensor by the gate that led to the changing rooms.

I walked over to the gate and did everything she told me. When I held the bracelet up to the sensor, it blared out a horrible noise that echoed through the lobby. A red X blinked on the screen. I tried pushing the gate, but it wouldn't open. It was icy to the touch.

A young man who, based on his outfit, seemed to be a pool employee, came over and asked me to hand him the bracelet. He waved it at the sensor in basically the exact same way I had, and with the same results. The alarm blared and a few tourists standing at the front desk covered their ears. The young man asked me to follow him to a glass gate next to the desk where he pushed a button and let me in.

'Hey – really sorry about that,' he said.

'No problem, it's fine,' I said. 'Totally fine – thanks.'

I wondered how much they spent on that machine. How long would that amount have covered the cost of paying a human being to stand there and take people's tickets? Probably a few years. Preferable, too, having a person there, given that the machine didn't even work.

In the changing rooms, I found a free locker with a number whose digits added up to ten, just like I used to do in the old days. I took off my old clothes. Back to square one, I thought as I looked up and saw myself in the full-length mirror not far from my locker. I was surprised at first, almost embarrassed, because I wasn't used to seeing myself naked at that distance. I felt like I was ogling someone else – some nude stranger. And then I saw how time had changed me. It was all too predictable; I was well on my way to becoming one of them, one of the naked old men sitting around me now, struggling to pull on their socks, gasping and wheezing like whales.

When I was a boy, we made fun of the guys who put their towels between their legs and pulled them back and forth to dry their crotches. Now I'd started seeing the practical value of drying yourself like that, even though it was inevitably comical. There's no two ways about it: it's uncomfortable being damp in places that don't air out. That's how you get funghi – and their attendant smells.

It wasn't possible to adjust the water temperature in the shower. When I was a boy, there were two taps – one with a blue dot for cold water, the other with a red one for hot – and thus you could adjust for the ideal temperature. They've adopted a new system since then. Now you press a knob under the shower head to get your allocated thirty seconds of tepid water. If you want more, you have to press the knob again. Of course, in the old days, someone was always forgetting to turn off the shower and the water ran, unused, down the drain until the pool attendant came and shut it off. This was obviously why they adopted the new system – to prevent waste and to make the pool attendants' job easier.

It didn't seem like the pool attendants had much to do. Two of them were sitting in their closet, fooling around on their phones and listening to the radio. Just a couple of boys. In the old days, the pool attendants were full-grown men who went into rages when we flung soap at one another or didn't wash well enough. These boylings who were the attendants now didn't seem likely to raise an eyebrow over anything, nor did they have the slightest bit of interest in whether people washed or not.

I put on my swimsuit and walked out of the shower. It surprised me that even though I hadn't been there in decades, I still took the most direct route to the hot pots without even thinking about it. I decided to start in the coolest pot, then go to the one that was a bit warmer, and thus work my way up to the hottest one. That's what my dad used to do when he was alive and for some reason, I've always copied him whenever there are different temperature hot pots. Less complicated that way.

There were a few men in the first hot pot, probably about my age. They were deep in conversation and from what I could tell, they were talking about the same international organisation that had been up for debate on the radio in the taxi. The men were clearly not in agreement about the facts of the matter and the discussion grew louder, faster and increasingly unintelligible until finally, it reached its apex and one of them stood up and lumbered out of the pot, ranting as he went. On the top step, he shouted the end of his speech – something about political movements and primary colours – before suddenly falling silent, slipping into his pool shoes, walking to the next hot pot, and getting in. No one spoke. The men who were left behind sat quietly for a moment but then started talking about something else, their voices calm.

It was then I realised that I knew one of them. His eyes and the shape of his mouth reminded me of a boy I'd played with as a child – even went to the pool with sometimes. But he'd definitely changed, if, indeed, it was him. The years had distorted him, his hair gone grey, his skin wizened liked pork crackling, his whole body just much bigger and puffier. Even his nose was swollen and bulging on the sides. His glasses were much the same, though.

Suddenly, our eyes met. I'd tempted fate, staring as long as I had.

'Don't I know you from somewhere?' asked the man.

'I don't think so,' I said.

The man took off his glasses, rinsed them in the hot water, put them back on, and peered at me.

'Wait, aren't you Elli? Elli Snæbjörnsson?'

'Oh yes, now I remember,' I said, attempting a smile.

'Don't you remember me? It's Einsi.'

'Yes, so it is.'

'Nice to run into you! How's it going?' asked Einsi.

'Yes, you too. Everything's great. How are you?' I said.

'Doing good, yeah. Yeah,' he said. 'You moved somewhere abroad, right? What were you doing again? Didn't you have some kind of software company?'

'Systems,' I said.

'What's that?'

'I design systems. For all sorts of companies.'

'Yeah, yeah. And you've just come back to the iceberg for a visit?' asked Einsi.

'Yes, and I've got some business here, too,' I answered.

'How are your folks?'

'Fine, really well.'

We didn't say anything for a moment. The sunlight danced on the ripples of the water, someone got into the pot and someone else got out. The water level remained virtually unchanged.

'I've got to get going,' I said, standing up.

'Good seeing you,' said the man.

'You too.'

'Have a good one.'

I got a bit of a headrush when I got out, even though the water really hadn't been all that hot. I decided to try swimming a few quick laps. I walked to the edge of the pool, jumped in, and sunk like a stone.

'Back to the iceberg.' I'd always found it an odd phrase. As if Iceland was literally made of ice, as if it were rootless, disconnected from the earth, adrift in the open sea until one day, it would finally melt away.

The Gardeners

Einar Már Guðmundsson

Translated by Victoria Cribb

As ANYONE WITH MORE than a passing interest in gardening will know, for a long time the very best gardeners here in the Greater Reykjavik area were displaced farmers. Some had moved to the city on the eve of the Second World War, following the outbreak of sheep rot that was ravaging the country in those years; others arrived during the war or just afterwards, as part of the great migration from the Icelandic countryside to the towns.

These days, although several decades have passed and this capable breed of men is fast dying off, there are still a few of them around, and they're considered in no way inferior to the younger generation of gardeners, who have learnt their trade at horticultural colleges at home or abroad.

This story is concerned with three such men, all brothers, from Skagafjördur in the north of Iceland. From father to son, for many generations, their ancestors had lived on a farm called Hvalnes, after the headland on which it stood in Skagavík Bay. The name is said to derive either from old tales of stranded whales or from the outcrops of basalt in the cliffs above the bay that are oddly reminiscent of whale's teeth.

The bay itself used to be a launching point for fishing boats; a proud settlement of seasonal huts had sprung up there, and in the early twentieth century it had been the site of a trading post and fish market. And once upon a time, back in the thirteenth century, more precisely in the midsummer of 1244, it had been the gathering place for the largest fleet in Iceland. Long-ships mobilised from all over the north of the country had assembled in the bay, and a formidable armed force, four-hundred strong, lay in wait there under the leadership of the chieftain Kolbeinn Arnórsson the Young.

Rarely has an invasion force like it been seen off the shores of Iceland. The plan was to harry the coast all the way from Skagavík to the West Fjords, and vanquish Thórdur kakali, Kolbeinn's most dangerous rival for control of the north. But the fleet which left harbour, heading for the Hornstrandir peninsula, got no further west than the neighbouring gulf of Húnaflói, where the forces of Thórdur and Kolbeinn clashed in the mightiest sea battle that has ever been waged in Icelandic waters.

More than three centuries later, at the end of the sixteenth century, around the time when William Shakespeare was sitting writing his plays and poems, an English ship went down outside the bay with the loss of all hands on board. A century after that, a Dutch ship, which had wandered off course, and which some believed to be laden with diamonds and other treasures, suffered the same fate. While in the late eighteenth century, as the sources tell us, a whole pack of hungry polar bears came charging into the bay and attacked the local women and children.

By the time the three brothers, Úlfar, Einar and Sölvi, named here in order of age, had grown to manhood and taken over the farm, there was little left to remind them of the glories of the past. No gallant fleets of long-lost heroes sailing across the bay, no fishing boats putting out to sea; both trading post and fish market had long since disappeared.

Then, as now, looking out from Hvalnes, which provides good shelter from the north wind, all that meets the eye is a succession of empty coves, as noble a sight on calm days in their mirror-like emptiness as when the wild surf rears up to meet the skies and the foam-capped breakers race onto the shore.

Then there's a singing under the soles of the feet, as if the old ships' crews were chanting or the sea itself were full of musical instruments. A dull throbbing passes through the ground, a faint, shivering vibration, while the old fishing huts, long reduced to grassy ruins, lie crumbling like ancient monuments, visited by none but the birds, and then mainly by the ravens, which perch on ledges in the curving cliff walls, gazing out with their black heads held high.

Like ancient sages.

Like unborn prophets.

Yet although the glamorous heroes of old had disappeared, except in the history books or in encounters with psychics, and fishermen and merchants from town no longer swaggered about the bay, the brothers were content in this harsh, barren landscape that lived deep within their souls and had etched its mark on their faces over the generations. Their life was here, where the grass grows best in the gaps between the rocks, and the sea ice comes visiting in summer.

Their mother had been able to trace her ancestry right back to the settlement of Iceland in the ninth century and from there back to court poets and Irish kings, and once, when the brothers were small boys, they had seen their father bring down a polar bear. They themselves had clubbed seals and plunged into icy pools in pursuit of trout, using nothing but their bare hands. Their livestock consisted of sheep and cattle, they had two decent little hay fields, and sometimes Einar and Sölvi rowed out to the fishing grounds. The brothers gathered up driftwood too and trimmed it to make fence posts, caught birds in snares on floating traps, and collected eggs and eiderdown.

If there was any downside to their existence, it was the lack of women: in the countryside, any number of handsome young men ended their days as ageing recluses. By the time the brothers got wind of any social gatherings, they were usually over. Nevertheless, in spite of this womanless quarantine, it never occurred to them to leave the farm, and they never would have done either if they hadn't been forced to when, one autumn shortly after the war, their sheep sheds and barn burnt to the ground.

They tried to build everything up again from scratch but then a hard winter set in. At times the snow was so thick that it blinded them and twice the gales seized every loose object and whirled it away. The locals watched as their tools and machines fell apart and a number of outhouses collapsed. Many farmers were faced with destitution as their livestock died of exposure or starvation, and a wave of calamities swept over the district. In quick succession, six unmarried solitary crofters gave up the ghost, a hard-working farmer was found dead in a ditch and three children died of exposure between one farm and the next. By the time the brothers upped and left, the only person still living in the district was the chairman of the local council.

But then other people arrived and now, long afterwards, there are at least thirty working farms in the area, and both a fish farm and a new harbour in the pipeline.

As no one will be surprised to hear, the farmers brought a variety of useful skills with them when they abandoned the land for the city. One of the things the brothers had in common with a handful of others was that they knew the art of building walls and windbreaks. They made outer walls either of stone, often with thin grassy turf strips between the courses, or entirely of turf blocks, which looked from a distance like a row of books on a shelf; the horizontal strips resembling shelves and the turf blocks the thick spines of books.

Today, such men are so rare that people scour the country for them. Their fingers possess a knowledge that has been lost. In their early twenties, the brothers had built the round sheepfold in Skagavík from blocks of lava, shaping each stone with hammer and chisel so precisely that when pieced together it was as if the blocks had been locked into place. After this, they had repaired the turf walls of the old church, almost building them up anew, so that now the church looks exactly as it would have done when it was built nearly 800 years ago.

So it was no problem for the brothers, once they began taking on gardening jobs in the city, to cut out pieces of turf or construct wooden frames, and still less to spread muck on grass or measure out plots of land, and, despite coming from an almost treeless district, to plant both hedges and saplings. Nor did it prove much of a stretch for them to create neat flowerbeds, raised lawns, flagpoles ringed with slabs of lava, or any of the other whims dictated by the modern age.

The only thing that struck them as strange at first was how the wide earth seemed suddenly to have shrunk to countless tiny housing plots. Before this, none of the brothers had ever visited the city, which was growing so fast in those days that later Einar said you could hardly blink without society undergoing some radical change.

As hill and moor beat a retreat, ghosts were dazzled by the light, and elves packed up and fled, new houses sprang out of the ground in so many places that no one thought it odd if small children believed the houses could walk or that the big blocks of flats were trolls that had been caught out on their long journey through the dark and turned to stone by the sunrise.

Surrounding all these new buildings were expanses of lifeless rock, the occasional huge boulder that would eventually have to be blown up, and wastelands of rusty nails, bits of timber, lengths of wire, torn cement sacks and spills of solidified concrete. The role of the brothers, and of others engaged in such work, was to convert these unpromising areas into neat lawns or even ornamental gardens. And so they got busy spreading out the topsoil dumped there by lorries, sowing seed, laying turf and planting.

Various people have pointed out the irony of displaced farmers working as gardeners, since although one can often find well-tended patches around farmhouses, gardening as such has never been a highly regarded occupation in the countryside. This is because, to a farmer, nature's beauty and usefulness are one and the same, whereas gardening reflects the mindset of those who do not make their living from the land.

Gardening, then, could be seen as comparable to landscape painting, which, historically speaking, did not come into existence until farmers had moved to the cities. Until then, the original – the landscape itself – sufficed. To hang it on the wall is, in the opinion of the true countryman, as foolish an undertaking as sitting of an evening, listening to recordings of his sheep.

Since it hadn't occurred to the brothers either that their rural skills might be useful in the city, or that working with grass could mean something other than the haymaking at home in Skagavík, they had all taken different jobs when they first arrived: Sölvi as a debt collector, Einar as a policeman and Úlfar as a mechanic in a workshop.

Sölvi, who couldn't find his way around the city, was always having trouble tracking down the people whose debts he was supposed to be calling in, and, as anyone who has ever worked as a debt collector in Reykjavik can imagine, things did not get any easier once the streets and house numbers had been found, and insults, anger and even punch-ups ensued. He used to come home with black eyes and a bloody nose, and once with the entire sleeve of his jacket missing.

While Sölvi was tramping the streets, calling in debts, Einar was working as an officer of the law, directing cars with a truncheon, since, much to his horror, he had found himself in the traffic division. During the rush hour, when the congestion was at its height, he would either flee to save his skin or else race after individual vehicles, yelling and shouting.

Only Úlfar found his job to his liking. As the eldest, he acted as spokesman for his brothers and felt responsible for their welfare. After giving the matter some thought, he realised what the problem was: the brothers needed to work together. It wasn't only their appearance – they were all ruddy, rough-hewn, burly and balding – that was similar, but their thoughts and movements were closely aligned as well.

Having come to this conclusion, and noticed all the plots of land that needed fertilising, Úlfar acquainted himself with how cars were bought and sold in the city, then arranged a meeting with a bank manager, took out a mortgage on the farm, and the next time he saw the American military base advertising an auction of vehicles at their surplus store, he took Einar and Sölvi along and they bought a sturdy jeep with a trailer.

After this, they purchased some tools and Úlfar put a small ad in the papers. In large print it announced: WE UNDERTAKE MUCK SPREADING, and in smaller print underneath he provided his and Einar's names, along with the telephone numbers of the workshop and police station respectively.

The demand far exceeded the brothers' expectations: it was spring and all the city's parks and gardens needed fertilising, but many people also got it into their heads that the police had expanded their activities and were engaging in a spot of muck spreading between shifts.

Phone calls came in from all the neighbouring districts and there were even requests from as far afield as up north as, all over the city, drunken humourists took to their phones and amused themselves at the brothers' expense. Luckily, all plans for legal proceedings were eventually dropped but Einar was dismissed from the force.

Úlfar and Sölvi immediately handed in their notice, as the brothers had more than enough to do with spreading organic waste and cow dung on the city's plots, and also in searching for accommodation, since the jeep they'd bought from the army had been so much cheaper than expected that, instead of paying back the rest of the loan to reduce their debt, they began ploughing through the advertisements for properties to rent.

The priority was to get out of the mildewed dump of a basement flat where they had been camping since they first arrived in town. It had no view and the only light came from a small window below a metal grating in the street. Sometimes they could see the mould crawling down the walls, and Sölvi had a permanent headache.

No sooner had an advertisement caught their eye than they were there on the doorstep: a large, wooden house, clad in corrugated iron, was for rent in the centre of town. *Space by arrangement,* was the exact wording in the paper.

Although the house turned out to be old and dilapidated, the advertisement hadn't lied about its size. It was a sunny evening. The brothers stood waiting on the steps, but for a long time nothing happened; all they could hear was the echo of their knocking indoors. Then there was a cough and the door began slowly to open. At first the brothers could see nothing but a pair of eyes in the gap. They stayed very still, waiting. Eventually, Úlfar said:

'Isn't this...?'

He got no further because at that moment the door opened wide, revealing in his entirety a dishevelled man with his flies undone. He was wearing a stripy pyjama jacket over a white vest, and a pair of crumpled, light-brown trousers that had never seen an iron. His face wore a weary pallor and, here and there, dark-grey stubble poked through his skin. The man turned and shuffled back inside in his slippers, inviting the brothers to follow him with an irritable jerk of the head.

In the sitting room, thick curtains blocked out the evening sunlight and a heavy fug of tobacco hung in the air; the floor around the table was littered with countless books, some lying face down, others with bookmarks between the pages, and in addition to these there were any number of periodicals, mostly in a large format with decorative titles. The table itself was completely buried in white sheets of paper, some scrawled all over with black ink, others containing nothing but short verses.

The brothers hovered on the threshold, peering round the half-closed white door into the room, with bemused eyes and gaping mouths, like trolls who have wandered into the wrong cave. Instead of speaking to them and asking what they wanted, the man sat down absent-mindedly at the table, picked up a half-smoked cigar from a green ashtray, lit it, and carried on busying himself with his papers.

He reached for a large book and started leafing through it, muttering under his breath in English, then wrote down a short verse on a piece of paper. After that, he drew a paper knife from the breast pocket of a dark jacket that hung over the back of his chair, aimed it and cut out several pages from a foreign periodical. The brothers had begun to clear their throats and cough into their hands, but the man didn't look up until he had put down the periodical and stubbed out his cigar.

'You still there?' he said. 'I thought you were only going to step inside for a minute.'

'We came...'

'Yes, you came, but I thought you'd gone. You must be after something?'

'We were sort of hoping to find out about the rent...'

'Oh, I just thought you must be cold.'

19

'It's actually quite a nice day outside.'

'It doesn't matter what the weather's like, around here most people are cold. If the cold doesn't come from outside, it comes from within.'

'Ah, I see what you mean.'

'If I'd meant something I'd have said it, but to be honest...' Up to now the man had been sitting at the table, but at this point, he got up and resumed, in a rather milder tone: 'Sorry, I wouldn't have spoken to you like that, but to be honest I thought at first that you were from the other side. Now, though, I can see perfectly well that you're from this side.'

The brothers made no reply to this, since they had no idea what the man was talking about. But he seemed unfazed by their confusion and added: 'Not that I'd have anything against renting to someone from the other side. It would just be a question of what currency to use.'

Later, when the letters started arriving, it dawned on the brothers exactly what the man had meant by his words, but that evening they didn't want to venture onto any thin ice as it was clear to them that they were dealing with a man of learning, so they simply introduced themselves when he came over, holding out his hand.

'Pétur,' he said three times, once to each of them in turn.

Next, he showed the brothers round the house where his father, a hard-working ship's captain, and his mother, a respectable housewife, had lived until their deaths, and later his wife until she'd left, which meant that Pétur, who taught at the secondary school in town, now had the entire house to himself.

To be free to do his academic work and preferably cut down his teaching hours, he needed to supplement his income by renting out as much of the house as possible. So he offered the brothers a deal that if they helped him move his belongings down to the basement, they could have both the ground floor and the attic to themselves.

The brothers accepted his offer gladly and have never had cause to regret it.

Although the brothers had plenty to do spreading organic waste and manure on the city's parks, verges and gardens, it wasn't long before they branched out. One day, as they were spreading muck on a grassy plot on the northern side of the Sudurland road, they were approached by a lawyer who had just had a large house built for himself.

The lawyer was tickled by the idea of being able to throw big garden parties like the lawyers abroad, and, after chatting with the brothers for a good while and getting an idea of their circumstances and what they could do, he invited them to build a turf wall along his drive and a windbreak at the northern end of his property, and once that was done he got them to complete the laying out of his garden.

The brothers, remembering the barren landscape up north, left some of the rocks in place and sowed grass seed in the soil between them, then planted trees here and there about the plot. Once the garden bloomed it was such a lovely sight that when the neighbours saw what a good job the brothers had done, they came to request their services too, and so it continued.

At home, meanwhile, they were sharing the kitchen with their landlord and, although they mostly rubbed along all right, there were two aspects of Pétur's behaviour that the brothers didn't entirely appreciate. One was his untidiness, the other his grumpiness. For example, Pétur never washed up and he had hardly been in the basement a week before the whole place was a mess. Periodicals, books, documents and papers spilled over everywhere and at times he would stand out on the steps, snorting, in such a foul temper that none of the brothers dared to speak to him for days on end.

No matter how much the brothers puzzled over the problem, they couldn't find any explanation for Pétur's peculiar behaviour, unless his divorce from his wife was to blame, since two years before they moved in, she had moved out.

But they were wrong.

As it happened, Pétur had had a good wife who had stood beside him and supported him in everything. But because of his obsession with his hobbies – medieval Icelandic poetry, on the one hand, and research into the development and structure of the English language, on the other – their communication had been strictly limited.

Sometimes Pétur wouldn't come to bed for weeks on end and it was only by chance that the couple ever ate a meal together. Sooner or later it was bound to happen: the woman fell in love with another man whose interests were neither as all-encompassing nor as time-consuming as Pétur's. When she broke the news to Pétur, he merely shrugged, so absorbed in his papers that by the time he looked up to say goodbye, his wife had gone.

When he had other things to do, Pétur saw no reason to wash up and he only changed his clothes when compelled to. But the chaos among his papers existed more in the eyes of others: in his mind, perfect order reigned.

It never took him more than half a minute to find a detail in a note or to look up a theory in an academic work. Every scrap of paper had its place. Under one table leg lay fragments from a commentary on the Old Icelandic poem *Völuspá*, or the 'Sibyl's Prophecy', while his English translations of the tenth-century poet Egill Skallagrímsson were to be found in the middle of the third pile of papers to the left, under his comments on *Beowulf* but on top of an essay about Sigurdur, slayer of the dragon Fáfnir.

His grumpiness, on the other hand...

It stemmed partly from his home-grown sorrows and those stuffy hours spent in semi-darkness, and partly from his frustration at having to waste his energies teaching grammar to numbskulls with no interest in the subject, instead of being able to devote himself to his research and his translations of the oldest and most precious pearls of Nordic poetry into the English tongue.

As if it wasn't bad enough that Pétur was bored with his teaching, his ability to find peace in the city was also diminishing by the day. So his interest was piqued when he heard the brothers talking of Hvalnes and the farmhouse that was still standing among the ruined sheds. In his imagination, he pictured an ancient seat of learning, heard the song of the sea, sensed the peace and quiet, and the more restless he became, the more he longed to be allowed to settle on the remote farm.

He wanted to escape the hubbub, leave behind the soulless city, and although the brothers warned him about the dark winter nights and the isolation that went with them, Pétur showed no signs of coming to his senses and wouldn't stop pestering them until the exchange had taken place.

The upshot was that the brothers kept the big house in the city, while Pétur moved to their old farm. The matter was settled with a reciprocal right of first refusal and unilateral inheritance rights, which would leave the brothers the eventual owners of both house and farm.

In the city, gardening was becoming ever more popular and before long a special committee was set up to reward the owners of beautiful, well-kept plots, and it did nothing to harm the brothers' reputation that on the first five occasions that owners received this type of recognition, it was for gardens designed and created by them.

It is no wonder, then, that the wording of the advertisement: WE UNDERTAKE MUCK SPREADING had, over the course of time, been adapted as appropriate to read: WE UNDERTAKE TO PERFECT YOUR PLOT, and so it has remained ever since.

Similarly, the telephone number provided in smaller print was neither that of the workshop nor of the police but, on the contrary, their own telephone number at their own address.

No sooner had Pétur gone than the brothers got to work on making radical improvements to the house. They tore off the roof and put on a new one, replaced the cladding and painted the whole house both inside and out. Meanwhile, as they were converting the surrounding sea of dock and steppe of weeds into a tidy garden, Pétur was toiling away up north, building a small byre with the help of craftsmen from the local town, and little by little acquiring twenty head of sheep, two cows and a dog.

In the summers, Pétur took on schoolboys from the local town to harvest the hay from one of the fields – the other had run wild – and to take care of the livestock and the milking. This left him free to attend to his academic research and translations of medieval texts, and, judging from his letters, he was pleased with this change of scene.

The wide-open spaces of land and sea suited him far better than the four walls of the classroom, and he achieved a much better rapport with his farm animals than he had with his secondary school pupils in the city. Not content with adopting the traditional Icelandic habit of christening his dog Snati and his cows Raudka and Skjalda, or 'Red' and 'Patch', Pétur gave names to every single one of his lambs and kept a book of ewes in which he wrote down every beast's distinguishing features beside its name.

As the brothers' fame grew in the gardening world, and they danced the old dances and became sought-after partners, Pétur got on with his writing and his farm work, and, if you leaf through his ewe-book and compare the dates, you can see that the day the brothers threw a tremendous bash to celebrate their joint wedding, Pétur was in the thick of the lambing, delivering one lamb after another with his own hands.

Before the postman in Skagavík knew what had hit him, he was lugging heavy loads of foreign periodicals and thick academic tomes to the remote farmhouse, and the brothers' fear that the dark winter nights and the accompanying isolation would weigh heavily on Pétur proved utterly unfounded. Besides, it soon transpired that Pétur was far from alone at the croft. According to his letters, he had a constant stream of visitors: old ship's crews were forever dropping by and ancient heroes often stuck their heads round the door.

It all began one evening when Pétur heard a noise from the kitchen and thought at first that the dog had knocked over a stool, but when this was followed by the sound of footsteps, he put down his pen and went to see what was going on. The dog was lying fast asleep in the hall between the kitchen and the front door, but nine Dutchmen were standing in a knot in the kitchen, dripping seawater all over the floor and gabbling away about something that Pétur, due to his limited knowledge of the language, couldn't quite follow.

He had an easier time later that month in understanding the Englishmen, who were inclined to be belligerent at first but were soon mollified when they heard what an impressive command this rough-haired, grey-bearded farmer had of their mother tongue. One of the sailors thought he must be home after almost four centuries in exile, and the most sensitive among them were moved to tears when Pétur started reading them the beautiful old poems he was working on. Back they came, eager to hear more. Pétur got various tips from them about his choice of vocabulary, and whenever he asked them questions they were quick to reply.

The brothers didn't believe everything they read in Pétur's letters; a few things struck them as downright odd. But the letters were always an occasion for reminiscing about old times, and they did whatever he asked them to. Pétur had other correspondents as well. One of these was Professor Haraldur Einarsson from the Department of Nordic Studies at the University of Texas. Pétur and Prof Haraldur had been exchanging letters for many years, and, for his part, Prof Haraldur was in no doubt about Pétur's academic judgement and regarded his translations of medieval poetry as second to none.

They also corresponded about personal matters. Pétur knew all about Prof Haraldur's arthritis and Prof Haraldur had been sent excerpts from Pétur's ewe-books and was aware that Pétur communed with long-dead ships' crews. Now it so happened that a dispute had arisen between three junior academics in the linguistics committee of which Prof Haraldur was a member. They were all specialists in sixteenth-century English and the controversy was about the extent to which William Shakespeare's plays reflected the everyday language of his times.

Three different opinions had been presented, and meeting after meeting had been dominated by heated rows on the subject. When Prof Haraldur, who had long ago lost patience with the endless wrangling, announced that all they needed to solve the dispute was a tape recorder, the other committee members had looked first at one another, then all turned to him, at which point he told them that up by the Arctic Circle there lived a farmer, scholar and translator, who enjoyed the privilege of being in direct communication with a ship's company from the exact period at the centre of the controversy.

The junior academics gaped in disbelief and some of the other committee members regarded Prof Haraldur with equal incredulity, but one man in the room, the head of the English Faculty at the University of Cambridge, couldn't forget his words. They went on buzzing in his ears and didn't stop bothering him until he had got back to England, written to Pétur and received his response.

Pétur provided a clear description of the sailors' language usage but was reluctant to make them talk into a tape recorder as he felt that this would be trespassing on the territory of psychics. However, he sent the head of faculty his translations of Old Icelandic poetry and also explained some of his ideas, all of this written in such faultless English that a decision was taken to invite Pétur to give a series of lectures at the University of Cambridge.

To the head of faculty, who was an admirer of William Morris, Pétur was living proof that ancient virtues, such as a thirst for knowledge and a boldness of ideas, could exist in remote places, even in the most abject poverty, and so great was his excitement that he personally led the delegation that was sent to convey the invitation to Pétur and witness for themselves the conditions in which he lived.

When the delegation arrived, Pétur was sitting outside in the farmyard, nursing an injured lamb; heavily bearded, in a torn shirt, with thin grey hair down to his shoulders. The delegation took photos and this was how Pétur appeared on the posters printed to advertise his lectures in the corridors of the university; an arresting image that caused many to stop and stare, and some decided to attend the lecture solely in order to get a good look at the man himself.

The people who turned up to gawp rather than listen to a primitive farmer delivering lectures about his English translations of Old Icelandic poetry were doomed to disappointment, just like the welcoming committee, who went to the airport to meet Pétur off the plane and failed to recognise the man standing there with his suitcase, peering around, in a light-grey suit, freshly trimmed and shaved, with a raincoat over his arm, looking exactly like one of them rather than the folklore figure they had invented for themselves.

The lectures went ahead anyway and in due course the brothers received a postcard from Cambridge. It said that the oil pump they had bought for him was working well and that he would reimburse them as soon as he got home. Perhaps Pétur had perceived the world as an idle, frivolous place. When he got back to the farm, he sat down and lit a cigar. It was to be his last. When the brothers didn't receive the customary letter at the appointed time, Úlfar went up north to check on him. And there he found Pétur, still sitting with a half-smoked cigar between his fingers.

Keep Sleeping, My Love

Andri Snær Magnason

Translated by Lytton Smith

YOU LOOKED BEAUTIFUL AS I left. I gently kissed your cheek, stroked a stray hair away from your face. I took pains not to wake you but it was so bright outside and I couldn't go back to sleep. My mind was aimlessly wandering; there was a weight on my chest. I wanted more than anything to slip the most beautiful word in your ear but I couldn't. I headed to the living room and opened the balcony door. Even there I couldn't find enough space to breathe so I pulled on my clothes and went outside. I started to walk but I still couldn't breathe – not on this street, not in this neighbourhood – so I went and got my bike and rode off.

The Miklabraut highway slopes west, so I started riding in that direction and right away knew where I needed to head. There was no traffic this early in the morning and I cycled in the middle of the road. I shifted into the highest gear and watched the lines on the tarmac run together as I stared down at them. If you've ever felt how freeing speed is with the wind in your hair you know there's no way you can stop at a red light so I just closed my eyes and didn't steer and held the handlebars tight and careened silently across the junction. The highway was like a dry riverbed and I had that awkward feeling a dried-up watercourse gives you, the suspicion that some force might break loose at any moment.

We've spent the same exact moment together every year: 9th August at 22:03. That's when the sun sets directly into the crater at the peak of Snæfellsjökull, a glacier-capped volcano. Since we first got together, we've watched this miraculous sight from the Grótta lighthouse, standing on the other end of a tombolo that floods during high tide. It's always so odd heading out west, past all the people dashing around town like they're missing out on something, but without the slightest idea what they're missing. It's truly amazing that we get this moment to ourselves. I've never met anyone else who has seen the sun go straight down into the glacier, even though it faces an entire city. I've never even seen a picture of it, and that makes the moment even more precious for us. Even when there's poor visibility and the glacier hides in the fog, at 22:03 without fail the mountain is there on the horizon, a black triangle outlined in gold, a sign of the coming darkness.

Nothing bad, exactly, has happened between us but things haven't been especially good recently. Yesterday I was out of sorts and the weather was a bit cold and damp so I said that the sunset was bound to be less beautiful today, that we should go tomorrow instead, even though it would be the 10th August and the sun wouldn't go right into the crater. Then you asked why I was taking this anniversary away and I answered that we were far too young to get fixated on some dumb nostalgia, that it would be okay to try something new, to see the sun set next to the glacier. You went silent and fell asleep.

Sleep is really the only thing we have in common nowadays. And yet it's been a long time since I dreamed of you.

We aren't alike. You decide on everything a long time in advance. I can never manage to decide anything until the day before. You can't ever jump at anything, you can't ever be spontaneous. If we don't buy tickets for a concert at least a week before, it's too late, we've missed it. But more and more frequently, I'll find myself saying, a day too late: 'We should have gone to this yesterday.' A year later, I can see all the possibilities that had stood before us – all the missed opportunities. You're trying to get me to decide something, to do something, trying to rouse us, but I always waste the moment. We waste each other's time and end up with nothing. My motto is always 'live in the moment' but I feel like I'm causing us to die off, to fade to zero.

When I was eleven, I was convinced there was going to be a nuclear war, if not right away then for sure before I turned fifteen. I have a memory of my sister and I sitting at home alone watching *The Day After*, a film about events following a nuclear attack. The A-bomb snapped a picture of the city with its white flash that blinded everyone and we sat there with our red eyes watching the shockwave ripple through the city. Burnt bodies sat in cars: Mum's dead body, Dad's dead body, their baby's dead body. Tires melted like they were margarine. I wondered whether my bedroom could stand such a shockwave, whether I'd get cancer from the radioactive fallout, and then I thought about the girl I had a crush on: would she survive? I came up with all kinds of rescue fantasies. I saw us together in the rubble, slurping down tinned food. I'd lend her my coat so she wouldn't freeze in the hell that was nuclear winter. And in its place, I'd get to snuggle up to her.

I'd barely gotten over the nuclear threat when the newspapers filled with stories about AIDS. Based on the reports, the epidemic seemed comparable to the black death, though it was too far away to truly scare me. Until the cover story in the newspaper: an AIDS patient had puked on the number 10 bus, the very same bus I took to school. I remember how over the next few days I didn't dare hold on to the bus's dangling black straps or touch the seat backs; everything had turned sticky and sickly. One time the bus stopped without warning and I fell down, scraping my hand. For a long time, I imagined that the virus had remained there on the floor from the vomit and seeped into my cuts.

On top of all that, the most popular YA books when I was twelve were *Fifteen Going Steady*, which told the story of a fifteen-year-old couple finding true love, and the sequel, *Sixteen Moving In,* about them renting an apartment and having a baby. All of this confirmed my suspicion that life ended at fifteen. Those books did, however, ignite my hope that just maybe I could get myself a girlfriend and start a family and make a home before we died of AIDS and a nuclear shockwave swept us away.

When I finally turned fifteen and the world was still standing as it always had, I wanted nothing to do with such conspiracies. Those YA books were the craziest things anyone had ever written; I forget the nuclear crisis for a while; AIDS was a distant thing. But because all of this was mixed up with puberty, I think the whole mess had a much greater impact on me than I cared to admit. Just as the ability to learn a language diminishes after puberty, it's like I've never matured enough to look beyond 1989, my fifteenth birthday. After that point, I only looked backwards. I went to school, but I had no idea what I was learning or what I wanted to do in the future. We got an apartment but not because of any plan or as a result of some grand decision. I was just going with the flow. Sometimes I feel like my soul hasn't realised I'm still alive, seven years after the imaginary end of the world, with ideas handed down from badly-written YA books, which were my only provisions for the journey into the future.

Perhaps it's ironic that when the world finally came crashing down, it wasn't thanks to a bomb or a virus but because of a word, and mostly because of what was going on inside me. That's why I've come here: I'm going to find The Word. And out of this new word, I'm going to shape a new world.

I cycled to the end of Hringbraut then down Eiðisgranda until the asphalt gave way to gravel and I got off my bike. I wandered about the headland, taking in the smell of the seaweed. It was low tide so I could get to the lighthouse. The arctic terns shrieked and the eider ducks scattered when I sat down where the two of us always sat, determined not to go back home until I had got to the bottom of myself and of love and you and whether these elements were meant to have any kind of connection at all. We've been together for a long time, an extremely long time if you ask my friends, incomprehensibly long. Thirty per cent of my life, half the time I have any memory of, most of secondary school, all of university. In reality, a seven-year relationship is not so complex when you fast-forward through it. If you're in love, seven years pass in no time at all.

Seven years had passed in no time.

But when your relationship stagnates, it's like the best part of your life has been spent on the couch, staring at films, the excitement of sex fizzled out. We squeeze onto the sofa and think that's how life is life, but we understand that everyone's lived a whole lifetime before us, and known a thousand people and had a million lovers, but we no longer know what is what. And now I'm back wondering about the past. Something inside me burns: can love leave room for any doubt? Can it say *maybe*? Must love be unconditional? Black or white, hot or cold: is there a tepid love? I've never been alone, not for longer than a week or two, and those times I always tried to hang out as much as possible with the guys or keep busy with school work. There's always something going on to fill up my eyes and ears. I've always mirrored myself on others, never given myself time to get to know myself, always trying to hold up my end of the bargain and do what others expect of me. I've never had to rescue myself. I've never gone travelling alone. I could do but I never do anything about it.

The first time we went to Grótta lighthouse on the 9th August, we didn't know what was coming, though we noticed the mountains at once. We marvelled at Móskarðshnjúkar, the three peaks between Esja and Skálafell. Mount Keilir was like a black pyramid in the wilderness and from a distance Snæfellsjökull was the perfect image of a volcano. All these mountains had clean, straight lines and sharp peaks: the only mountains near the capital that look like the mountains children draw. Sometimes, I like to think mathematically and calculate my position in the world based on these mountains. We were in the middle of a circle which passed through Keilir at 120 degrees and Móskarðshnjúkar at 240 degrees, with Snæfellsjökull at 360 degrees – and right then the sun disappeared straight down into its crater. It was all too cool to be a coincidence. The mountains were there precisely because of us.

I'd always been fascinated by those mysterious places ancient nations left behind. I'd read about shrines that had been built for just one sunset a year. That evening, we got a place like that ourselves. In a history book we'd read, there had been a picture of Nefertiti looking strikingly like you in profile. We imagined Keilir as your pyramid. As beautiful and as flawless as you, black as the soft triangle below your navel.

I was Móskarðshnjúkar, which is formed out of light rock, making it always seem like a ray of sunlight's shining at the peak. I was like that, optimistic and good-natured and hair light as rhyolite. But I was also scattered, divided in three like its three peaks.

Then there was Snæfellsjökull; that was the love within this ring.

The second time we went out to Grótta on the 9th August, it was low tide so we walked over the sandy isthmus to watch the sun descend into the glacier. When we went to head back the land had flooded again so we were stranded. We knocked on the lighthouse door but there was no one there, we were totally alone in the world. No one could reach us and no one could see us except the arctic terns, so we took off our clothes and made out with our toes in the grass at the foot of the lighthouse. The mountains came together as one in the circle's middle.

In this perfect circle, the glacier volcano stood for love. This natural wonder took on the character of law in our minds, it was self-evidently true. It was a worldview no one doubted. But one day I found an old map and thought to draw a circle on it and see if we'd calculated accurately. Amazingly, Móskarðshnjúkar and Keilir were exactly in a circle with its radius in Grótta, but as for Snæfellsjökull? It was far outside the circle, like where the asshole might be. Where the glacier should have been stood: nothing.

It occurred to me that maybe it had all been a hollow illusion. That this combination of friendship, curiosity, excitement, discovery, touching, laughter, youth, belief and sex was something different than we'd thought. Maybe love doesn't tolerate being measured and verified. Maybe that causes it to retreat the way a glacier retreats.

I sat there on my own under the lighthouse and grew cold. Suddenly I felt I had no right to be there at the circle's centre without you. Especially on that particular night, stealing our 22:03 moment. The answer was surely to be found on the gold peaks that lay on a bearing of 240 degrees. I locked up my bike and rang a cab.

A white Mercedes Benz came and carried me off towards those peaks. The driver tried to be upbeat, talking cheerily about life. He must have seen how preoccupied I was, how defenceless, out on this headland surrounded by ocean. I asked him to take the sea road, Sæbrautin, because I didn't want to have to look at Keilir. When the car sped past the black central bank building with the oil tanks at Örfirisey on the left, and Móskarðshnjúkarnir visible to the east, I felt confident about the errand I was headed on. I was going to find a new Word.

Counterfeiters are thrown in jail because they produce too much money, undermining the economy by causing currency to lose value. But who resists when the dearest words in our language depreciate? Icelandic phrases like *ég elska þig* sound more and more like the weaker 'I love you,' a phrase that has long since lost all meaning. 'I love you' doesn't mean much more than 'I like spending time with you' or even 'see you soon' and often 'nothing'. Every time you *love* to eat ice cream, or you *love* Toyotas or *love* pizza, the value of the word drops and we find we need to add more and more adjectives so we can speak our minds. Teenagers use the word up on their first dates; people print it on t-shirts; finally, it becomes a cliché that is useless for everyone. How to express your deepest feelings when a word itself has become meaningless? When it's been severed from its association with the heart, connected instead to plastic hearts and to chocolate?

I'd written an essay back in primary school and when the teacher returned it, it had a stamp on it: FINE. That was the highest score you could get but I still protested the ruling. No matter what the teacher tried, even though he stamped a smiley face next to the word, it never sat right with me. To me, 'fine' was as good as 'passable.' The teacher was trying to pay me in an obsolete currency. We'd had newer and better words for a long time: very good, great, awesome, crazy.

What do we do once *ég elska þig* becomes as meaningless as fine, as passable, as 'I love you'? The heart's left with nothing but coins that are out of circulation. I 0.0000000 love you. What can we use instead?

To the best of my knowledge, my nana has never said that word. But I know it's alive inside her, that she treasures it like a jewel: the word shines from her eyes. It was a big decision when I said *ég elska þig* for the first time. I tried to conceal it inside when I felt it coming. But the word sought a way out and spoke itself wholeheartedly. It was odd to feel such a strong emotion inside me and to share it with the outside world – to describe everything going on inside in a single word.

It was so good to have that word in my mouth, *elska*. It was sleek and wriggled like a fish, I felt it swim through my veins and along my nerves and stretch them out, and then I set it free in your ear and it swam around your brain and it must have tickled you because you laughed and clenched around my thighs. I cried when you paid me back with the very same coin.

Yet most beautiful of all was when you kept the word in your eyes, where it was blue in colour.

The word stands out like a red sock in a white wash.

A long time later, I'd just returned from the movies with the guys and there was a frostiness between us for some reason I can't remember now, and we did it without kissing or anything beforehand, and when I was all done I said *ég elska þig* but you said that I only said that when we did it and you turned your back on me. 'Come on,' I said, 'You know I love you.' But I wasn't sure.

After that, I couldn't say anything nice to you without seeing the word you kept in your eyes and I saw in them something else you didn't say: not true. Your eyes were grey and everything I said was so inflated that the noughts piled up next to important words like air bubbles getting into the bloodstream, killing my heart every time I said *elska*.

I was the one who'd destroyed the word, connected it to things other than the heart. I was sceptical about us during a difficult time but I wasn't brave enough, to be honest. You clearly weren't feeling any doubt because you did not spare the word and I used it to answer you, not wanting to hurt you. I felt all those noughts burning when I said it, so I started avoiding the word and simply saying 'you too' or 'likewise.' When the feeling finally returned, whole and pure, I felt like

I couldn't use the word again, that it brought back up those times I'd faked it.

I'd been a counterfeiter. I'd printed the word on fake paper, weakened its value. I burned.

My heart is covered with cold copper.

In the beginning was the verb *að elska*: to love. It existed before me and a heart formed around the word, one that sprouted and formed a brain that was green like a turtle and it grew a shell around it that is my face.

I have to find a new word. Only then will I be whole again. It'll be a word no one can use in car commercials. A word that will never be printed on Valentine's Day cards. It will only exist between us.

The car carried me along the road that leads up to Mosfellssveit and rattled along a gravel path past a few cottages, until the driver stopped on a hillock above a stream that trickled beneath an old footbridge.

'You okay, mate?' asked the cab driver, with a concerned stare.

'Sure.'

'What are you up to?'

'Just hiking to the summit,' I said.

'You sure you're alright?' he asked.

'Yes.'

'You feeling a bit off?' he asked.

'Exactly,' I said as I paid.

'You're not going to do anything, are you?' he asked.

'Like what?' I asked.

'You know,' he said.

'Not if I can find the Word,' I said.

'What word?' he asked.

'A new word that creates a new world.'

I walked down the road to the stream, not bothering to cross the wooden bridge but hopping over the stones to the far bank. The car sat there idling for a bit until I heard the engine pulling slowly away.

The peaks rose into the sky like those childhood mountains, golden like the sun, though the grass growing on the slopes shone green. I wondered if it was possible to love mountains. If it was possible to love a mountain, it must be possible to love a hill and a cliff and even a rock. It would have to be a very beautiful rock.

It's not a given that the word *elska* sounds innately good, that its heart, '*lsk*,' touches your heart more than any other word. Say it fast and repeatedly and it shifts: *elskaelskaelskaelskaelskaillska*, loveloveloveloveloveloveevil.

Evil. *Illska*.

The word I'm looking for does not contain a bit of evil.

The girl I'd hoped to meet up with after the nuclear war was called Lilja. I'd cuddle up to my bedroom wall at night or wrap myself around my blanket like I was hugging her, but I kept my feelings to myself until I felt I couldn't any longer and then I would hide inside the closet with a red Sharpie and my schoolbag. Inside it was some loose card that contained a white plastic pocket where I put all the words that were trying to find a way out of me.

The new word will be expansive enough for all this because love is child-like and innocent.

Lilja was a year younger, incredibly beautiful and she had a red dog. I walked past her house many times a day hoping to catch a glance of her through the kitchen window. One day, I came across the red dog on my way home from gymnastics. I grabbed the bull by the horns, so to speak, and chased the red dog across the whole of Elliðaárdalur Valley. I brought him home to her and rang the bell but as soon as I did, I heard barking from inside, her red dog barking, and I turned red, too.

The new word will need to contain this feeling, too, because love is pubescent and stupid.

On my way to school, I'd cut across a grassy meadow; it was autumn and it was covered in frost. I noticed there were these little knobs round about and I realised there was a group of sleeping golden plovers. They were all around me, their heads under their wings, the whole field covered with them. I stood stock still, knowing that to walk through a field of sleeping golden plovers was something worth living for.

The new word will be full of sleeping plovers.

You, above all, will need to fit inside this word. It'll contain every single memory of you and every single word we've exchanged. The word must be blue when it shines in our eyes; it will need to tickle our brains each time we set it free. It must hold every kiss and each and every touch and it must grow as we grow.

The word should colour our future the way red threads through white laundry.

I climb up through the heather and up through the grass, through moss and dirt and gravel, I crawl up yellow scree until I reach the peak. An actual peak.

I lie on my back and look up. I see nothing but blue and I hear nothing but the noise of the wind. Beyond the peak, there's a valley with a winding brook and if I can't find the word I can walk down into the valley and over to the next peak and make myself disappear behind that mountain.

I close my eyes and cover my ears and hold my breath. I listen to the rumblings of the machinery that drives the body and I think about all the things over which I have no control: my heart that keeps beating and my lungs filling with air and I try to think nothing, try to think nothing at all and to imagine how the first thought came into being. Then it's like I hear something roaring or whispering and when I listen harder, I sense a word there. I measure it against my heart and it fits so well I feel like I might burst. This word is so big it swallows everything I can see. Like a blank page on which a child draws

the sun
clouds
mountains
a waterfall
birds
water
fire

The word is so simple and so beautiful that it feels like it has always been in my heart.

I feel like I need to speak it aloud.

I'll whisper it to you when I get home.

Home

Fríða Ísberg

Translated by Larissa Kyzer

YOU DECIDE TO WALK. It's July and the weather's nice, the city tinted a twilight grey in the early hours of the morning. You glance at your phone. It's 3:14am. You tally up how much you spent tonight. Maybe you were smart and stopped drinking after your third beer. Maybe you stopped drinking at 1am. Maybe you've got work in the morning. You look like you're around the age where you're still pulling weekend shifts in a restaurant or café. Maybe you ended the night by chugging the last of many beers – you're not the kind of girl who lets half a pint go to waste, even if all your friends are heading out the door, even if your wingwoman has found a suitable someone for the night.

You look at your phone again and stick it in your pocket. Grasp your keyring in your other one, thread your fingers through the keys and clench your fist. A ready-made mace tucked inside your trench coat. It makes you feel better, even if you don't really know anything about self-defence. Are you supposed to punch your attacker right in the face or swing your fist around like a cat with its claws out? You make a mental note to ask YouTube when you get home.

Home. How long to get home? You map out the walk in your mind, chart a rough course in advance, taking into account what streets are narrow and shadowy in the half-light and what streets are wide, well-lit, and well-trafficked. At some point, you're going to have to take a deserted street that's lined by tall hedges. Your best friend's little sister was attacked on a street like that. Or maybe it was your best friend herself. You never take that street after dark. And there's another one you never go down anymore, either, even though it's the most direct route home, since you found out a girl was attacked there a couple of years ago. It was in the news. The attacker threw her against a wall and was tearing at her pants and she screamed and he ran off. You're not sure how loud you could scream. Or whether you could scream at all, really. Maybe that would be a good thing to practice sometime.

You take out your phone. You want to call someone. Wish you had a boyfriend waiting for you at home. Maybe you do have a boyfriend at home in bed, but you don't want to wake him up over something so trivial. You wonder if any of your friends would mind staying on the phone with you while you walk home, even though you just spent the entire night together. Your wingwoman is busy, of course.

You scroll aimlessly through your phone contacts as if you're focused on something other than the gardens you're walking past. The ones someone could drag you into. You hover over your mum's number. She would understand, even though she obviously went to bed ages ago. She wouldn't like knowing you're downtown by yourself, has often asked you to call when you get home if she knows you're going out. You always need to reassure her that there's nothing to worry about, that you'll be careful, you never drink too much and you always try to walk home with someone else. She likes to bring up the attempted attack a few months ago, or how many assaults are reported annually and how there are more every year. You always answer that it's not the number of assaults that have gone up, but reports. These days, women are more likely to seek help after being assaulted because there's greater public awareness. Sometimes, you've no choice but to firmly end the discussion, say goodbye in the same voice you'd use to tell a dog to sit, toss your hair over your shoulder and decide that you're not going to let your life be dictated by would-be rapists. Go out on Saturday night, get drunk. But in the back of your mind, sprouts the seed she planted when she told you her story. In the back of your mind lurks the secret you promised you'd never tell anyone, ever. That she was. Under what circumstances, it makes no difference, nor how old she was when it happened. Just that she was. That knowledge is why you stopped rolling your eyes. Her warnings took root in you, instead of going in one ear and straight out the other.

You notice a man about half a block away. He's walking on the same side of the street, coming right at you, pretty fast. Unusually fast? You clench your fist tightly around your keyring. Move your hand up and down to make sure that you won't have any problem getting your fist out. That the keys won't get caught in your coat pocket. He's rapidly approaching you. You squeeze your phone in your other pocket. Pull it out as though someone's calling you. Enter 999 just to have it ready. Pretend to answer. You look up from the ground and then down again. He's noticed you. He's about twenty metres away now. I'm almost home, you say into your phone, and yeah, I had a good time. You say it loud enough that he can hear you. He steps into the street and crosses to the other side. You watch him in your periphery. Throw a quick glance over your shoulder a few steps later. See that he's well down the street; he's not going to jump you from behind. It occurs to you that maybe he crossed the street specifically so you wouldn't have to be afraid.

You're still ten minutes from home. You regret not taking a taxi. You just live right at this embarrassing middle distance, a fifteen-minute walk from downtown. Far enough that you want to take a taxi, but close enough that you don't really have an excuse to. Younger and poorer you would have never even considered it. You think back on all the times you walked home in those days, how you drank, how you took drinks from anyone who offered, how you'd pad home in just your socks, unsuspecting, unconcerned, sometimes two nights in a row on weekends. You realise how lucky you are that nothing ever happened.

You've arrived at a major road. A few taxis drive past. You relax a little, even though it's still twilight and there aren't many people out. You mentally prepare yourself for the final stretch. The hedgerows. Find yourself suddenly thinking about a conversation you had with a friend a few months ago. You were at a bar and there was this guy who'd been watching you for a long time. Hovered around you like a little moon. Never got too close. He wasn't one of those puffy-eyed, thick-tongued older men who try to buy you a drink and then just stumbles off when you give him a look. This guy had his shoulders thrown back, his eyes were focused. Sweaty palms. Something off about him. When you started pulling on your coat, he sidled up to you and asked if you'd like to go to his place. You could feel his loathing. It scared you. Your friend had cycled there; you were on foot. You asked him to walk, to take a detour with you. It was cold – this was right between winter and spring – and he was reluctant, didn't understand what the big deal was. Made a joke about you being paranoid, then gave in. You promised to invite him over for pancakes the next day, which you forgot to do. 'Don't you ever get uncomfortable walking home by yourself?' you asked when you arrived in your neighbourhood. 'In Reykjavik?' he asked, sceptically. Looked around the empty street as if to show you how harmless it was.

You hear the crunch of leaves. There's someone behind you. Right behind you. You hear it, all of a sudden. Quick, short steps. You pick up the pace and hear them speed up, too. You steel yourself for an attack as you turn around.

It's another girl. She's a little younger than you. Not dressed for the weather at all. She looks a little drunk. She smiles at you. You can breathe easy. There are two of you. No one's going to attack two women. You smile back, a bit ashamed of your heart, pounding in your chest. You both walk not-together for a while. Then you have to turn onto another street. She continues straight ahead, arms crossed under her breasts, shoulders spiked and stiff like a big M. She's walking a lot faster now. Stumbles over the uneven sidewalk but quickly regains her balance. You're gripped by a sudden rage. That you're both this scared. There was a time when you would have listened to music on your way home. Turned it all the way up, even though it made your headphones buzz. Your quick steps become angry strides. You've turned onto the street with hedgerows, with cut-throughs, back alleys, and tall trees. There's no one around. You feel like taking all your clothes off and strolling the rest of the way naked. Taking your time. Swinging your ass as sexily as you can. Stroking rings around your nipples with your Fuck-you fingers.

You're almost there. Your house is two minutes away. You decide to take a cut-through; it'll be even quicker. You feel like you've sobered up, but that's probably not true. You try to remember what you have in the fridge. Did you eat that frozen pizza?

Probably. You don't look like the kind of girl who'd forget she had a pizza in the freezer.

There's your building. You unclench your fingers so that your fist-mace turns back into a palm and keys in your pocket. You pull out your keyring. Find the front door key. It has purple or yellow rubber around the edge. Or maybe it's one of those old-fashioned gilded keys that are shaped like a trapezoid. Your sidewalk is strewn with gravel. There are your stairs, leading up to your front door. There's a flower in a tin can on each step that the woman who lives next door decided should live there, too. You've made it to the door. You open it quickly and step inside. Close it behind you. Double-check the doorknob. It's locked. You sigh. You're relieved. You're home.

Two Foxes

Björn Halldórsson

Translated by Larissa Kyzer

THE SUN HAD YET to rise, but the night was so brilliantly white behind the flimsy curtains that he couldn't sleep. His wife was dreaming peacefully on her side of the bed. He found, with unexpected bitterness, that he envied her. It was so easy for her. She was out the moment her head hit the pillow. Every night, she fell asleep beside him on the couch while they were watching TV. Usually, he'd wake her up when it was time to go to bed, but he'd stopped of late. Instead, he brushed his teeth, crawled under the duvet, lay in the darkness, and waited. After a few hours, the bedroom door would creak, and he'd feel a weight on the other side of the mattress as she slipped into bed without touching him. This was their new routine. Him with his eyes closed and her with her back to him, knees drawn up to her chest. Lying there in the darkness, he wished she'd cuddle up to him, scold him for leaving her there on the couch and tell him to wake her up from now on. It was only once she got into bed that he could sleep. Or usually that did the trick, but these bright summer nights were killing him. For the last week, he'd lain wide awake until morning and then stumbled through the next day like a sleepwalker.

He sat up and swung his bare feet onto the cold floor. He wouldn't be sleeping anymore tonight. He paused at the foot of the bed and gazed at the duvet's hilly landscape, his wife hidden underneath. The only part of her that was visible was a tuft of hair, sticking out from under the covers. Short hair, almost a buzz cut. A frumpy, old lady cut. When they got married, she had hair down to the small of her back, which was the style back then. He'd tried to drop hints, without being pushy, that maybe she should grow it out again. She said it was too much of a hassle to brush and style and wash, not to mention what she spent on dyeing the roots. No, short hair was much easier. She didn't understand how she'd ever bothered with such vanity.

'At least now it doesn't tickle your face in bed. You were always complaining about that,' she said.

He didn't doubt she was right, but he couldn't remember it having ever really bothered him. He must have said so at some point. Women remembered what you said, the good and the bad. Declarations of love you didn't think you'd ever expressed, cutting retorts you couldn't remember having uttered out loud. They stored them all up and trotted them out when they needed to remind you who you were. Or, at least, who you were at one point. He nudged around with his toes until he happened upon his slippers, put on his robe, and closed the bedroom door silently behind him.

He turned on the tap in the kitchen. While he let the water run, he gazed out the window at the moss-covered lava field that surrounded the house, imagining what it would feel like to press his palms into that dewy greenery. They almost never made love anymore, even before this new silence settled over them. Only occasionally, as if out of habit. As if they were suddenly embarrassed around one another. Embarrassed by their old, worn-out bodies, their soft folds and stretch marks. She turned around now to take off her bra and underwear before putting on her nightdress in the evening. In those moments when she stood naked with her back to him, he would stare at her, but as soon as she turned around, he'd look away, ashamed of his lust and cowardice.

The water ran cold. He drank straight from the tap and then filled a glass. Hidden under the sink was a pack of cigarettes, along with a lighter and a jar he used as an ashtray. He stuck the jar and cigarettes into the pocket of his robe and stepped out onto the deck. The cold went straight through the thin soles of his slippers. Outside, there was a large propane grill, plastic garden furniture, and a hot tub.

They lived in a new development in the middle of a lava field that was created in an eruption thousands of years ago, the lava hissing and slithering its way from a nearby crater all the way down to the sea. The lava had heaped up in hideous crags along the shore that must have inspired tales of trolls in the old days. The streets in the neighbourhood were paved, but there were still no sidewalks or traffic signs, although the city had installed heads on most of the streetlamps and run electricity to them. He and his wife started building at the same time as a handful of soon-to-be neighbours. That was before the crash. Afterwards, almost everyone had stopped or delayed construction until finally, they were the only ones left. All of the surrounding lots were tied up in legal disputes due to underwater loans. No one would be building here any time soon. In some places, a foundation had been poured, with maybe a wall here and there. Rusty hammers and planks on sawhorses were strewn around, as if the carpenters had all thrown down their tools and raced off to other, more pressing jobs. But most of the lots were vacant, their driveways leading straight out into the lava. In the glow of the streetlamps, it looked as though the houses had simply floated away one after the other, vanishing behind the clouds.

He flopped down into a chair, set his water glass on a table and carefully shook a cigarette free from the nearly full pack, tapping the filter to pack the tobacco. He'd bought the pack the other day on a whim. The lighter crackled. He drew the smoke deep into his lungs and slumped back in his chair as the nicotine hit his bloodstream, feeling himself relax even as his heart beat faster.

The deck faced the sea and those peculiar cliffs standing like sentinels along the shoreline. The house was pretty big for just the two of them but having spent half their lives in a closet downtown, they liked being able to spread out. Out here, they had plenty of outdoor space for grilling, high ceilings and south-facing windows that ensured they always got some light, even during the dark days of winter. When they'd first settled on the blueprints with the architect, they'd had certain ideas about what they'd do with the two extra rooms, but when they finally moved in, it felt like they'd missed their moment. He couldn't say with any certainty which one of them had made the decision. They turned the extra bedrooms into an office and guest room.

They bought a beautiful quilt for the guest bed and a couple of colourful pillows that collected dust at the headboard. The pillows were impulse buys and the only things from IKEA in the whole house. They spared no expense on the new decor, went on countless expeditions to expensive furniture stores that, before this, they'd never have thought to set foot in, picked out a sleek, designer sofa, decorative footstools and other incidentals. It would, after all, be their last home. The kitchen had all the top-of-the-line gadgets, all in red, as per the colour scheme. Red and white in the kitchen, autumnal colours in the living room and master bedroom, sea green in the bathroom. The bathroom had two sinks and they commissioned a much-in-demand craftsman to create a mosaic on the wall. The tile shards were in all different shades of green and the mosaicist took pains to ensure that the design was completely random, with no discernible pattern.

All their work paid off. They even got a feature in *House & Home*. Two double-spreads. Glossy pictures of the living room and bathroom and kitchen and deck – everything but the laundry and garage and them. There were no pictures of them.

They'd thrown out or given away all of the furnishings from their old apartment on Kárastígur. He could barely remember what they'd had there – just a bunch of old junk that had amassed over the years.

He exhaled a cloud of smoke and snorted. Tapped ash off the end of his cigarette. Took another drag. Leaned back in his chair and looked out at the lava through half-closed eyes. Other than some bird chatter in the distance and the crackle of his cigarette, it was totally silent. Something caught his eye; the moss was moving. He peered through the smoke. A patch of landscape was flitting back and forth out in the lava field, disappearing into fissures and reappearing once again. It stopped now and then, as if in thought, before padding cautiously closer. A pair of eyes was observing the house.

He'd only once before seen a fox in the wild, back when he was a boy, hiking with his parents. They were walking into a narrow valley in the Westfjords when at the top of the next ridge, they caught sight of little grey puffballs, wriggling in the sunshine.

'Look!' said his mother. She hung her binoculars around his neck and pointed him in the right direction. 'Do you see them?'

Fox cubs, just emerged from their burrow. A vixen lay on a stone some distance away, keeping watch. He looked through the binoculars at the cubs tussling like little boys until their mother noticed the interlopers, yipped, and one by one, took her young by the scruff and tossed them into their den. When he and his parents got there, there was no trace of the little family, but he'd seen the burrow's entrance through the binoculars. He lay down in the grass and peered into it. His father grabbed his arm and yanked him sharply to his feet, leaving behind a bruise the size of a ten krónur coin.

'Have you lost your mind, lad?' his father hissed. 'You can't be dangling your fingers in there! They'll bite and not let go until the bone snaps.' He grabbed his son's index and middle fingers and squeezed until the boy whimpered in pain. Then he let go, horrified and shamefaced. His father had grown up in the Eastfjords and as a child had seen lambs with their faces torn apart and eyes hanging out of their sockets. Had heard the piteous bleating of a ewe that couldn't find her lambs. He'd learned from a young age to hate minks and foxes the way that only a farmer could, seeing in them a cruelty that city kids could not conceive of.

'If I'd had a rifle,' said his father later that same night, sitting at the entrance of the tent and stirring a mug of hot chocolate with the knife he kept on his belt whenever they went camping. 'If I'd had a rifle, I would have shot her and her cubs, too. Foxes should be shot on sight, just like minks. Any time they run across livestock, they go into a frenzy and don't stop until they've killed everything they can sink their teeth into.' He shook a few extra marshmallows into the steaming mug and passed it to his son where he sat curled up in his sleeping bag. His mother was inside the tent, reading by the light of her headlamp. His parents had been short with one another since they'd encountered the vixen and he felt like his father was really talking to her when he dried his knife on the hem of his shirt and said: 'Normal creatures aren't like that.'

The fox was brown and about the size of a cat. The animal had paused on the bottom step, paw warily outstretched over the clean lines of the deck.

'Good day to you, sir,' he said to the fox. His voice was dry and cracked. He cleared his throat and repeated the greeting.

The fox, naturally, didn't reply but sat in the moss, blinking at him. Its eyes were different than those of a dog or any other domestic animal he'd known. Yellow and disinterested, as though it knew that its destiny and that of the man were two separate worlds that would never overlap.

'Am I bothering you?' he asked the fox. Odd that it didn't run away. He'd always heard that foxes kept their distance from people and would hide if they caught so much as a whiff of man. Maybe they've gotten used to us, he thought, now that our city is encroaching upon their wilderness.

'I have nothing for you,' he said lamely, but the fox kept staring at him. He smoked the rest of his cigarette in companionable silence, relaxed the muscles that had tensed up when he saw the predator, inclined his head towards the fox and watched the smoke curling from the tip of his cigarette and out into the white night. Something was happening beyond the horizon. There was an orange glow over the ocean. He heard a gabbling in the lava and then a long, woeful cry.

'Someone misses you,' he said to the fox. It turned its head in the direction of the sound, stood up and trotted away without even looking over its shoulder by way of parting. He watched the little brown pelt skittering between the hollows and over crevices until it faded into the landscape.

'Nice to meet you, too,' he said jokingly to the horizon. 'Give my regards to your missus.' He caught a glimpse of two shadows silhouetted by the sea and merging into one just as the white membrane stretched across the sky dissolved in the rising sun. Its rays poured over everything, leaving spots on his retinas.

The cigarette burned down to the filter, stinking of burning plastic and he got a queasy feeling as he stubbed it out. He tried to contain the reek in the jar, but he knew it would stick to him. He took a gulp of water to relieve his nausea and swished it around his mouth, spitting over the railing and pouring the remainder into the moss. Inside, he hid his shame under the kitchen sink and refilled the glass.

She was awake; he could sense it as soon as he entered the room.

'Where'd you go?' Her voice was low and heavy with sleep.

'Just out for some air,' he whispered. 'Couldn't sleep.' He held up the glass. 'I got some water. Would you like some?'

She lifted herself up and reached out blindly with one hand. She held the other over her eyes to block out the light.

'It's so bright,' she whispered.

'I know. We need heavier curtains.' He tried to give her the glass, but her fumbling hand couldn't find it, so he gently took hold of her wrist and guided it into her grasp. The coil springs in the mattress groaned when he sat down.

She took a sip of water and handed it back to him. He reached across and put it on her nightstand.

'You keep it. I've had enough.' They lay back down.

'Were you smoking?'

'Yes, sorry.'

'Don't apologise,' she whispered. 'It was your choice to quit.'

'I know, but I do want to quit.' I don't want to die, he thought. I want to live a long life with you. She turned towards him, and he froze, petrified that he'd been speaking out loud.

'Your shirt smells of smoke.'

'Sorry.'

'It's fine. I remember a time when you always smelled of smoke.'

They lay still and silent for a moment. He listened to her breathing and tried to hear if she'd fallen asleep.

'Sorry I woke you,' he whispered, not expecting an answer.

She pulled the cover up over her ear and cheek, trying to hide from the daylight for just a little bit longer. 'I don't like sleeping without you.'

'No,' he whispered. 'Me neither. Without you.' He wondered if she'd remember this conversation when she woke up.

'Sorry,' he whispered again, but she didn't answer, had fallen back asleep. Not long after, so did he.

Without You, I'm Half

Kristín Eiríksdóttir

Translated by Larissa Kyzer

OUTSIDE, A STORM WAS raging, a rubbish bin had been blown over and was clanking along the pavement. In the apartment, water was simmering, piano music was playing quietly and, every so often, the wind could be heard gnashing in the plywood walls. Hafliði tallied up the sounds and then got up to spoon some coffee into the cafetière, waiting a few seconds for the water to come to a boil before pouring it over the grounds. He knew drinking coffee this late was unadvisable, and he also knew that there was almost no chance that the house wouldn't be able to withstand the weather. That the roof would be ripped off and sail out into oblivion with him and all his loose odds and ends.

It was about as unlikely as an aeroplane crashing on top of him as it flew low over downtown Reykjavik on its way to the airport. And yet, this is exactly what he always felt was about to happen whenever he heard the rumblings of a storm or plane overhead. Likewise, he sometimes felt certain that the house would collapse around him even though it was dead calm outside. His mind would drift to earthquakes and suddenly, he'd see the bearing piles crumble, clear as day. He'd thought a lot about the best place for him to be in the event of a collapse. About whether it'd be better to be upstairs or down.

Would it be more practical to be on the ground floor, so he'd have a quicker route outside, or would it maybe be better to be higher up, so as to avoid being crushed by all that weight? Most likely, it'd be best to be lying in his bed with his mattress underneath him, and that was, indeed, where he spent most of his time when his mind started assaulting him with thoughts of building collapse.

When the coffee was ready, he walked over to the window and looked out onto the street below. It was after midnight on a Saturday, but even so, there was no one out on Laugavegur – the weather was too bad. He himself had backed out of a dinner party invite and was starting to regret it. He wanted to go to a bar, but it wasn't impossible that he'd run into someone who'd been at the dinner party. No matter what bar he picked, you could never rule it out. And it didn't bear thinking about what would happen if he ran into someone from the party. The thought was like a bog he sunk into without being able to offer the slightest resistance.

A few girls emerged from the snowfall, wrapped in big scarves and hats, although they all seemed to be bare-legged and wearing heels. Giggling, they swatted playfully at each other, falling over as they did and he thought of Ástríður, the girl he suspected was at the dinner party, wondered if she'd gone and if she had a boyfriend. He thought that maybe the host, Beta, had been plotting something to do with the two of them.

He'd run into Beta about a week ago at a coffeehouse. They'd been deep in conversation about plant life on the ocean floor. Hafliði was talking about how trawlers destroyed the seabed with their fishing tackle, and the consequences that had for the earth's ecosystem. Beta was really into environmental protection and, to be honest, knew more about the subject than he did. They were sitting by the window that faced the intersection of Njálsgata and Frakkastígur and, even though

Hafliði was listening attentively to everything Beta was saying, he still took note of a girl passing by. She was striding purposefully down Njálsgata, straight-backed and stately. On her head, she wore a silvery turban, out from under which flowed long, thick hair that was exactly the same white as the faux fur coat she had on.

The girl was tall, broad-featured, and, at first glance, not particularly pretty. Hafliði meant to point her out and say something sarcastic, but Beta beat him to it, knocking on the window to get the girl's attention. She waved gleefully, giving a strange little strangled cry that died abruptly when she realised that the girl couldn't hear her through the glass. 'Ástríður!' she said, glowing, then got to her feet as the girl, who'd now come into the coffeehouse, threw herself around Beta's neck. They kissed and squealed and when the celebratory shrieking was over, Beta invited her to sit at their table, much to Hafliði's annoyance, as it had been a long time since he last saw Beta and he hadn't come close to telling her everything he wanted to. While the girl got herself a coffee, Beta explained that Ástríður was her childhood friend and had just moved home to Iceland after living in Amsterdam for a long time. Hafliði asked if maybe he shouldn't take off so they could talk, but Beta wouldn't hear of it.

Ástríður came back with her coffee, set it on the table, and took off her coat, under which she was wearing what appeared to be an old-fashioned diving costume. A tight orange jumpsuit made of some sort of rubbery material. Her breasts were large, and her neck was conspicuously long. Hafliði took her hand, introduced himself, and she smiled at him with her whole face, each tiny muscle put to work in its service, her steel-grey eyes glinting a particularly white white. It also didn't escape his attention how white her teeth were – they protruded, glancingly white and large, from her Barbie-pink gums. How strange it seemed that this woman was thirty years old – that she and Beta were the same age. She must be, in that they were childhood friends, but compared to her, Beta now seemed grey and sickly, drawn even, and a little worse for wear. He'd never thought about his friend this way before.

Ástríður was soft-spoken and shy, much to Hafliði's surprise. Quite to the contrary, Beta was talkative and funny, cracking jokes as if it were second nature to her as the other two listened, laughed, and egged her on. When Ástríður finished her coffee, she excused herself, said she'd been on her way to visit her grandmother in the nursing home. Then, she smiled that smile at Hafliði and when she was gone, he felt as though she'd sprinkled him with glitter. Beta sighed and rested her chin on her palm.

'This happens every time I run into her,' she said, shaking her head. 'She appears and suddenly I'm fun, like magic. For a long time, I thought *she* was the fun one, but then I realised that she never says a word. Not a single word!' Beta started laughing and Hafliði said she was absolutely right – Ástríður had been silent while Beta talked and talked – and then hurriedly added that the way Ástríður dressed was, all things considered, funny enough in itself. Beta looked offended and he immediately regretted what he'd said.

'She's always dressed like a bozo,' Beta responded with a laugh. 'She's *so brilliant,*' she added, and then started telling Hafliði stories about when they were teenagers. He'd heard most of them but before, Beta always said *my friend*. Now, her friend had a face and a name. Beta told him how Ástríður had studied herbal medicine in the Netherlands. She'd worked at some sort of special clinic abroad but was planning on doing something completely different now; she'd grown tired of it. That's the way it went with everything she did – she'd get obsessed with some fad and then lose all interest in it. Do in two years what other people would spend their whole lives pottering away at. Before this, she'd been in a techno band

and had raced yachts or something like that. Hafliði could hear an edge of jealousy to her voice and decided to shrug, as if he hadn't been totally enchanted by her. Which, as it happened, was a lie.

They got back on course after that, kept yammering away like always. But Hafliði noticed that Beta was distracted when they said their goodbyes, maybe even a little upset, he thought. As if some painful thought had just occurred to her.

The next day, Beta called him and invited him over for dinner. He accepted and they chatted for a bit. Just as he was saying goodbye, she asked him to wait, was quiet for a moment, and then asked what he'd thought of her friend, Ástríður. It caught him off-guard but in the end, he said she seemed lovely. Beta hmm'ed and he felt like she was about to say something else, but she rang off.

It reminded Hafliði of being in sixth form, of the way girls had called him up and asked him to go out with their friends. No, he'd always answered and hung up, even if he had a crush on the girl in question. The thought of mute cinema dates and miscalculated kisses were enough to make him shudder. Now, he was starting to feel anxious about the dinner party. He was convinced that this Ástríður would be there, that she was behind the whole thing, that she was using it to trap him. Which in and of itself, he had nothing against. She could toss him over her shoulder and march him home, have her way with him and then throw him out after. It was all the other stuff he found difficult – what his part was supposed to be in the whole thing. All the possible slips of the tongue and clumsiness that he'd been guilty of, again and again, his whole life. He was filled with self-pity and the dinner party loomed over him, maw gaping, and cast a shadow on each intervening day until he woke up on Saturday and heard the storm outside his window.

More and more people were starting to appear on Laugavegur, in direct proportion to their alcohol consumption, he thought.

Being drunk makes you immune to the cold. He poured some cheap whiskey in a glass – whiskey he'd bought to take to the dinner party, in fact, and two bottles of red wine besides. Bottles that were now standing on his kitchen table, still in a plastic bag, and made him feel uneasy. Like a gift for someone who'd died unexpectedly before their birthday, he thought, entirely aware of how dramatic the comparison was. He'd always thought there was something utterly tragic about gifts. Maybe because his grandma died barely two weeks after her birthday, and when he and his dad went to collect her things from the nursing home, he'd found the soft, pink scarf he'd given her. There it was, lying folded in its wrapping paper, and he'd bawled his eyes out, the first time he'd cried since he got the news of his grandmother's death. This was when he was a teenager.

No matter how cheerful the occasion, he always felt slightly depressed when he picked out a gift for someone. Things are so cruel, he thought, so soulless and, in most cases, useless. CDs that no one listened to or that immediately got scratched at the birthday party, figurines that wound up in storage and then broke the next time you moved house. Kitchen gadgets that only made meal prep more complicated, pictures that would be ripped out of their frames and exchanged for new ones. Books whose spines were never cracked. Ill-fitting clothes and scarves on top of scarves, great heaping piles of scarves.

He imagined Ástríður's suitcases, the ones she must have brought back with her from Amsterdam, and how colourful and playful their contents. He envisioned a gold-flowered hookah with a violet bowl, gumballs bouncing all over the place when she pulled out a neon green dress. Glitter dusted around her grandma's room at the nursing home. He lay on the couch with his laptop on his stomach and opened his email, drained his glass of whiskey and sipped on cold coffee. He realised suddenly that the storm had died down, that outside it was calm. He went back to the window and looked out on

Laugavegur, heard the ruckus of people going out of bars or in, or else loitering, ID-less, outside, just standing there and smoking.

There was a group of teenage boys in his line of sight and Haflíði watched them curiously. They were passing a bottle back and forth, spitting constantly and yelling, voices cracking, at one another and girls passing by. When he was their age – not so many years ago – he carried his cousin's ID in his wallet and always got into clubs and bars whenever he used it. He also used it to buy alcohol at the Vínbúð. He was always the one who did the buying for everyone before school dances. It was at one such a dance that he met his first girlfriend, Magga. He was just drunk enough to get through their first conversation, kiss, and, later that night, his first sexual experience without incident. The day after, he made the most of his hangover stupor, and chatted with her late into the afternoon. Her parents were away, and they were lying on the living room floor. There was a snowstorm outside, not unlike now.

She was a stern-faced girl, stubborn and solitary. Her limbs were stout, her skin oily; she often complained about the sweat marks she got on her shirts and the dark down that grew on her upper lip. She thought she was fat, too, and once, when Haflíði said she was soft, she was so hurt that she left, even though it was the middle of the night. Haflíði thought she was soft and beautiful. When they broke up a few weeks later, he was so depressed that he lost his appetite, was perpetually on the verge of tears, and nearly passed out in gym class. He quickly forgot how happy he'd been with Magga and wrote off the entire experience as terrible. The whole thing had been a failure – hopeless and typical for him. He was just that kind of person.

He was in a few brief relationships after that, the longest of which ended after six months. He'd met her at university, where she was studying geology.

One time, when they were talking about their childhoods, she told him a cute anecdote about a parrot and Hafliði told her a long, dramatic story about something that happened to him once in the countryside. Something about a dog and a lamb with a cleft palate that had to be slaughtered. The girl listened attentively and when the story was over, she said she thought it was funny how much he made of everything.

'Something that would have been no big deal to me,' she said, 'you experience as some great tragedy. I totally get that you've had troubles, but still: you've got a great family, you do well in school, you want for nothing. Why do you always act like it's a miracle you survived? I mean, what's actually happened to you? Other than life, I mean. We all have to survive *that*. Sometimes I think you're missing a few layers of skin!'

Not so long after that conversation, Hafliði went over to her place and said he wanted them to be friends. He didn't like her like that anymore and when she put her head in her hands and cried on the couch, he laid a palm on her back and felt like the whole thing was unreal. The girl was just one more couch cushion that dissolved into nothing as the walls crumbled around them. The entire house, the earth, and him, just drifted, disembodied, out into nothingness.

The night that girl told him he was missing a few layers of skin, Hafliði got upset and called her a common pleb, said it depressed him the way she trivialised and oversimplified all the things that made human beings remarkable. It bored him, he said, how unimaginative she was, acting like people could only be *this* or *that*. He didn't exactly understand why it made him so mad. He got pins and needles all over and wanted, more than anything, to fling himself out the window. And then he got scared. Windows became his enemy; the thought of allowing himself to clamber out of one and splotch down onto the asphalt below was never far away. It huddled behind all his other thoughts, slimy and hostile, like an organ on the verge of bursting.

A patrol car pulled up alongside the group of boys and they walked off. The car continued slowly down Laugavegur and for a moment, everything was silent. Haflidi went to the bathroom and brushed his teeth, flossed until his gums were streaked with red and then went to bed.

His room was windowless and just big enough for a single bed. He'd built a shelf over it on which he'd arranged a lamp and a pile of books, his diary on top. Every evening, he went over his day, writing up the smallest details in a chronological narrative, and when he woke up, he tilled his memory for dreams and tried to record them in the same fashion. The latter was more difficult, especially when he first woke up. Sometimes, he called Beta first thing in the morning and read her the dreams he'd written down. She kept her phone on her nightstand, and would reach over and answer it, halfway between sleep and waking. Haflidi would recite his dreams in her ears and then hear nothing, she'd have drifted off, so he'd hang up. It was something she'd come up with and Haflidi thought it was a bit strange. Beta got strange ideas sometimes and Haflidi didn't always understand them. Wasn't sure what she wanted from him. Or why she wanted to hear his dreams while she was half-asleep herself.

They'd met the night he broke up with his last girlfriend. He'd said his shamefaced goodbye while she sat there, head still in her hands. Later, standing on the street outside her house, he felt oddly good. He pictured a strand of electrified DNA, the chain-pattern of his body illuminated and crackling, and he walked to the Vínbúð whistling. Went to a party and drank more than usual, talked faster. The words spitting out of his mouth sounded exotic to his ears, laden with meaning that was just beyond his own understanding. The more he talked, the closer he felt he was getting to some sort of meaning. As if he were travelling through a dense jungle, sword flashing, cleaving plants and boughs in two. He didn't usually enjoy the sound of his own voice but that evening, no one else could get a word in.

Hafliði didn't remember how he ended up at the same table as Beta. His friends had disappeared and then, all of a sudden, he was sitting next to her. The bar closed and everyone who was still there went over to her place. A few others joined along the way. She was wearing her leather jacket and a short, striped dress. Her hair was up in a big, messy knot on top of her head. She had a neon yellow purse around her waist, the kind that tourists wear, and in it, she kept her cigarettes and a little tin filled with coke. There was a picture of a kitten on the lid and every now and then, she took it out, stuck a guitar pick into the powder, and held it under the nose of anyone who wanted some.

She reminded Hafliði of the type of girl you saw so often in '90s movies: a hellion who spontaneously starts dancing or flits about in a giant, old Cadillac; barefoot in acid-washed jeans and see-through tank tops, whimpering as she walks into the surf; unlucky in love, sitting on the back of a motorcycle, resting her cheek on some violent lout's back and them rumbling along a mountain road in California, her perm blowing out straight behind her in the wind.

Everything changed after Hafliði met her. His old friends seemed childish and unexciting and things that were important before now didn't matter in the least. Like whether he finished college, for example. He'd always done well in science, so he'd enrolled in engineering at the university right after he'd finished upper secondary. He was in his first year when he met Beta and stopped going to classes not long after the semester began.

On his birthday – his 21st – Beta gave him a book by Pessóa. It was in English and called *The Book of Disquiet*. He untied the blue ribbon around it and ran his fingers over the crumpled paperback. Beta said Pessóa was her favourite poet. Haflidi was touched to receive a book that she herself had owned, read, and held in her hands. He thought about her as he read, where she'd been when she'd read this poem or that. He imagined her in different scenarios, in different colour outfits and hairdos at differing levels of weird. He astonished his parents one night after dinner at their place by leaving with a stack of books under his arm. The collected works of Einar Ben and Steinn Steinarr. Classics his parents had inherited. They teased him and his dad said he hoped Haflidi hadn't started writing poetry. His mother gave him a quick elbow to the ribs when he said this, in the event that was indeed the case. Which, of course, it was. Haflidi scrawled them in the back of his diary and hoped they were better than he thought they were.

He sat in bed as Saturday night rolled into Sunday morning, writing. The calm continued unabated and the only sounds he heard were from Laugavegur: techno music from cars creeping slowly along the street, couples fighting. Glass breaking and angry shouts blending with bursts of laughter. It was 3am, then 4am. His mobile phone rang from the living room. It was loud and he jumped, sat frozen in bed and waited for the ringing to stop. Haflidi got up, found his phone, and saw an unknown number. He looked it up in the online directory, but it was unregistered. When it rang itself out the second time, his heart started beating rapidly and he began pacing around the living room. Then it rang a third time and he answered tentatively.

'Haflidi?' asked an indistinct woman's voice. He didn't recognise it.

'Who is this?' he asked, and he heard a clatter on the other end of the line, as if the speaker had dropped the phone on the floor.

'Who is this?' he repeated.

'Is that you?' said the voice and it now sounded like she was a long way away. He didn't answer, just listened to a strange noise, a long suctiony sound and something that might be stifled tears.

'Without you, I'm half,' he heard the voice say, but he couldn't be sure. The sucking sound got louder, like a powerful gust of wind, and the connection was lost.

Reykjavik Nights

Auður Jónsdóttir

Translated by Meg Matich

THE PUBLISHER WELCOMED ME to her home behind Hallgrimskirkja in a blue bathrobe with a pattern right out of the 1960s. Earlier that week, she had won the Nordic Council Literature Prize, and so she was still extravagantly tired after days of celebrating, Scandinavian-style.

The warm smell of breakfast filled the air – Danish sausages and cheese, and the classic Icelandic prawn salad. White candles were lit as if to counterpoint the frigid wind outside, and the room felt comfortably dreary as we both sat down. She told me that I could smoke out of the window in the kitchen, knowing that I'd recently taken up the habit again – my husband of eighteen years and I had divorced, and with our parting, I'd also left the house that I'd known all my adult life.

'What's new?' she asked, a smile lighting up her face. She'd tied her dark hair back, drawing attention to her hypnotic eyes. Relative to your typical Reykjaviker, she was otherworldly – raised in Belgium and France, her mind steeped in books and dramaturgy – and she was always quick to spot the theatrical in life's forward motion.

'I've stopped acting like a teenager,' I said, and she shot me a sardonic smile – she's 45, too, and had also attempted to leave her husband and marital home. Like so many of my friends these days; educated, mature women who woke up in a world they didn't recognise, and felt compelled to consider who they were after so many years spent institutionalised by marriage. Discovering what it means to be in a marriage, what it means to be out of one. Eager to find their feet, but anxious – like me.

'Still, I'm glad I got to try it out,' I continued. 'Being a teenager again. Your inner teenager is your true self, I think.'

'How's that?' she asked in a deliberately sultry voice. Not because she didn't know what I meant, but because she wanted to hear more about my inner teenager.

'All this chaos,' I said. 'Understanding at this age is just as elusive as when I was a fourteen-year-old girl, except this time around, I know that there isn't a recipe for living.'

'No, there certainly isn't,' she snickered wearily, but seemed excited to hear more. 'Oh, well!' she sighed, glutted on Danish cheese, Icelandic prawn salad and the blue Capri's we smoked after we ate.

'Tell me something,' she said.

'Like what?' I said.

'Something about this inner teenager of yours,' she pressed.

'Oh, the travails of a middle-aged woman in Reykjavik?'

'Yes,' she said, itching for a juicy story and a cigarette.

'Okay,' I said. And so I began.

'I went to a bar.' That's how the story starts.

She settled down into her seat and repeated back to me: 'You went to a bar?'

I told her I'd bumped into one of our mutual friends there, who was with another friend I didn't know. The friend was cute, a tall guy with crow-black hair, who'd just moved back from Barcelona. He was pretty drunk and keyed up. As if he were uncomfortable in his own skin.

'Why?' she asked.

'Because he'd just separated from his partner and his stomach was full of sadness and he was just stumbling. In chaos. Like me.'

'And?'

'And he tried to get with me like some plastered guy who's out of his mind with grief. Grasping at straws for any sort of intimacy. He was so pushy that my friend started to apologise for him. It was a mess, a complete mess. But still. A drowning man's thirst.'

'Intimacy,' she weighed up the word.

'Yeah, because when you get to that point, you'll do anything for a little closeness,' I said. 'If you're drunk enough.'

'Even you?' she asked.

'Yes, even me. I hadn't slept with anybody in over two months and my sex drive was stoked with liquor.'

She smiled with the full comprehension of a woman who has at one time or another tried being single and drunk on a night out in Reykjavik. She listened, greedily. I told her about how I'd gone home with the man in question.

On the way home, I asked him if separation was so bad? 'Yes,' he said, his raspy voice breaking. 'Oh yes, it's really bad!'

He looked emptily out into the night, the wind whipping its way towards us. Then, he shouted: 'You have to save me!'

I'd intended to heat up some milk for him, cover him with a blanket, and let him – at most – cuddle me while he slept. He seemed so delicate, with fine features and tragedy in his eyes – then he let out a conspicuous laugh. He needed to hold onto somebody, anybody, and to fall asleep. Suddenly I was very much awake. Instead of just sleeping together, we really slept together.

I kissed him goodbye in front of the Polish builders who were tearing apart my bathroom at the behest of my landlord. Crawled back under the covers and slept until the builders began to drill. And then I started to feel awful.

What the hell had I done? And who was I?

A woman in a nightgown, with dark curls damp from the rain; a nose still slightly crooked from getting punched in the face at a party when she was seventeen. Now she's 45 and has started partying again. She's so newly divorced that she tore the sheets off her bed and hadn't bothered to replace them before going out to obliterate herself. So apathetic that she still slept on a mattress on the floor in a rented flat.

She'd intended to vacuum for the last two weeks but put it off because of the renovations in the bathroom. It would hardly take any effort. Yet dust settled over everything.

There, in the shocking light of day, the dust bunnies were the size of rats. The clean laundry lay scattered across the floor. This place was temporary; her actual place was in another country. And she smelled of this man that she didn't know. And the bathroom looked like a car park under construction. She wasn't a woman; she was a freak. Shame settled toxic on her body.

'The shame of women,' I said to the publisher who was carefully smoking out the window.

'Sex and garbage,' the publisher said, squirming with delight.

'It was a recipe for toxic shame,' I sigh, squatting inside my own self-reproach.

But the writer inside me came to the rescue; she asked around for his email address. She wrote him an email in florid prose to make the shame disappear.

But she didn't quite know what she was doing. She only knew how to be honest with her husband. To say what needed to be said. And she used that experience to put it all on paper: she wasn't a slut, though going home with her that night must've been like a trip to the smoky boudoir of a whore. Her things were in another country now and the builders were at work and she didn't quite know why she had taken him home when he was in such a vulnerable state, but she hoped that he was alright and, well, he was hard even though the sex was sloppy and just… she hoped she hadn't been too careless with him.

Her maternal heart hammered as she wrote. Yes, she was writing to try and clarify everything – to clarify something that she herself didn't really understand – her, a shame-filled mother who suddenly found herself in a sexual situation in her own home, amidst chaos. Who was she? What did the words on the page even mean? She wasn't sure but continued to write in search of an answer. Words, words, more words… poor tools for analysing the circumstances. Just a few months before, when she had still been cut off from the world in the pleasantly predictable cell of marriage, she never would have suspected she would find herself here.

The words were the only thing that she had, so she hit send.

And the email, its pure and white surface now a rat's nest of black words fraught with shame, garbage, and the memory of such incoherently sad sex, found its way to some office somewhere in the city where a man she didn't know sat – still naked in the haze of her memory. What would her ex say about her behaviour? He would be appalled.

And honestly, the grieving man would be, too. No answer came.

A few days later, she sat across from a psychologist, a middle-aged man at a practice in central Reykjavik. She acknowledged that she felt unsettled because she had tried to efface her shame with words, but her email hadn't been acknowledged.

'I didn't mean anything by it,' she said. 'I just wanted to explain… that I wasn't a slut.'

'This type of vulnerability – sending this man an essay – doesn't invite actual closeness,' the psychologist said. She eyed him mistrustfully before saying: 'But that's me! I'm an author! I write long emails.'

'If you want society to accept you, you have to behave within the parameters it sets,' he said unblinking as he made a note on his legal pad. Probably something about a crazy woman who has trouble with intimacy, she thought as her insides cringed.

After the session, she stepped dejectedly into the uncomfortably bright day. Downtown brimmed with life – tourists and white-collar workers, all the usual prattling figures, and then her.

Abnormal. Sixty-nine kilos of shame. Flesh and stinking words. She'd been infected by the man during sex, infected with the need to claw out of her own skin.

That was until Teddy and Twinkie came flying from Paris. Twinkie was her French translator, who was well-known in literary circles. Teddy, Twinkie's partner, worked at a French bank, but was nevertheless well-regarded.

They stayed with her for a few nights and exfoliated the shame with humour and well-intended but tenuous analogies, cassoulet, champagne, and forbidden French cigarettes. Then a third friend arrived in the grey gales of Reykjavik. An American Jew based in Israel, who had won numerous awards for his fearless writing and was more into men than women, even though he found it easier to live with women. He'd tried both – first living with a woman and then a man. Split up with both.

They went to meet him at Kaffi Paris; Twinkie who looked just like himself, Teddy who looked just like a teddy bear, and her, with her rain-wet, windswept hair, dark and peppered with greys, and her too-big chest. She wore a wool sweater like she was seventeen again. But her third friend was fashionably dressed in a luxurious blouse, with a boyish haircut, and a constant inner glow. Brimming with life, meaning, desire, and daring – like his books. We called him Lust. Lust said, without the least trace of embarrassment, that he had always been a little in love with teddy bears, prompting the broad-shouldered Teddy to fiddle proudly with his black beard and the beardless, slender Twinkie to smile proudly, too.

Lust was in the process of founding an LGBTQ+ literary festival in Tel Aviv, and had recently been offered a bodyguard. He said he'd become accustomed to the fact that his love life provoked the outside world. And then he told them about divorce culture in Israel; in a nutshell, divorcing meant moving to Tel Aviv to let yourself go wild for a year or so. He offered to buy a bottle of white wine for the table. She ordered herself a coffee, watched waiters courier bottles in ice buckets to and from the table. They toasted and laughed at the fact that they were listening to Dolly Parton in a French coffeehouse in Reykjavik.

The wine, mixed with strong coffee, put them in a wildly romantic mood, and they decided to trade stories of recklessness and danger. She told them about the man who had waded through laundry up to his knees to sleep with her on a mattress on the floor, and how she had written a long, messy email to him, and how that email had made her an outcast from the very society that carried on as usual outside the window where they sat.

'Oh,' Lust gasped, crossing his hands over his chest so that his palms pressed against his nipples. 'I would love that!'

'Love what?' she asked, unsure.

'I would love it if somebody would write me an essay after sex!' he sang out, with all the sincerity of somebody possessed by Dolly Parton. He shook his head, overjoyed, and winked at her in admiration.

'Essay!' I said to the publisher, who was now crying through laughter and smoke. I wrote an Essay After Sex and I loved myself for it – I loved myself after he said that. Only wish I'd written a longer one. And a messier one. A Real Essay!

She smiled: 'Yet you say that the words didn't void the shame.'

'The right words,' I clarified.

'Did you meet him again?' she asked.

'He crawled back to his wife. I was a pick-me-up in the middle of a marital tiff,' I said, taking another cigarette. 'Rekindled the whole thing. I've seen them together and I really am happy to see him happy. Being divorced and middle-aged is so disorienting.'

'Like fumbling in the dark.'

She knew the feeling because she'd tried it out herself – and found closeness, friendships, and most importantly, love. Not to mention, strength. Even though we – women who have gone through divorce – grumble about the prison of marriage, when all is said and done, we understand that it's complicated to protect yourself for your own sake. And you may feel threadbare and defenceless, but you're still linked to the deepest parts of yourself. And when you face trials, you also go through a sort of enlightenment.

'But,' said my book-loving friend, who sees the bigger picture better than anyone I know, 'that thing about society needing to affirm you…'

'Yeah,' I said, tensing up.

'It's not a question of being accepted; it's just that you don't fit into *this* society,' she continued, drawing out her words as if savouring her own conclusion. 'Your home isn't really among the good citizens of Reykjavik, but in the queer Jewish community in Tel Aviv.'

She handed me a brand-new book, still smelling of hot ink as we parted. With a sense of closure, I went out into the luminous, ashen day. When all is said and done, life, more than anything, is a juicy story.

Incursion

Þórarinn Eldjárn

Translated by Philip Roughton

WHEN THE LUMBERYARD CLOSED for good, the buildings and storage sheds, the drying loft and workshop, were all dismantled. The big brick smokestack was knocked to the ground and the turret with its cupola was taken down; a young wholesaler bought it and now uses it as a garden shed, people say. The lot was subdivided and sold to real-estate developers. A number of high-rise buildings then sprang up like mushrooms, and suddenly one spring, the first residents had moved in. They could be seen drifting behind their windows, like happy fish in an aquarium. They would be looking down and up at the watercolour glory: the screen-blue strait, green islands afloat, Mount Esja in the background.

Next, a bakery came to life on the ground floor of one building, and on fair-weather days, its aroma drifted among the buildings and in through open windows. Therewith, all the premises for a beautiful life seemed to be fulfilled.

But then it was as if a kind of misfortune began to haunt the place: the building contractor went bankrupt. He turned out to have lost all the money that people had paid into their apartments. No assets were found in his name, not even the house that he lived in or the Jaguar that he drove – both of which happened to belong to his wife. Most of the apartments were half-completed, and one building was shell-only. So now, all further construction was halted; no one else moved in and the shell-only building became a ghost house the first autumn and winter.

The few people who had had their apartments handed over to them could thank their lucky stars. Despite the unfinished state of the development overall, in their case, being left high and dry was a blessing.

But their good fortune didn't last long: the place was truly haunted. When spring came anew, unidentifiable sounds began to be heard. Most prominent was an odd whining, machine-like noise early in the mornings and strange clunks and thuds from time to time throughout the day, sounds that seemed at a glance to have no natural explanation.

Little by little, these mysterious sounds began to grow louder. Eventually, the noise kept everyone in the building from getting a wink of sleep after about four-thirty in the morning.

Now the race was on to find the cause of this commotion, and soon, after certain knowledgeable individuals were questioned at length, it came to light that the whining sound was surprisingly reminiscent of the one that the big table saw in the workshop used to make, while the clunks and thuds were alarmingly similar to those made back in the day when the lumber was being stacked.

An expert on psychic phenomena was called upon, and he came to the conclusion that the noises were being made by deceased employees of the Lumberyard, who were taking the disappearance of their former workplace quite badly. The ruckus itself should be taken as remarkable proof of the fact that machines could become ghosts, no less than men. The expert was convinced that this was also the reason for the bad luck that plagued the contractor and the residents.

The parapsychologist recommended holding a special Homeowner's Association séance, at which every attempt would be made to come to terms with the deceased. The HOA began preparing for just such a meeting, and among other things, asked a former employee of the workshop to provide information about his departed co-workers. The idea was, by these means, to come to a better understanding of whom they were dealing with, and thereby be able to predict both which of the deceased might be expected to appear and what their demands might be.

But when the problem was described to the old employee, he said straightaway: 'Oof, this doesn't have anything to do with ghosts. It's the starlings.'

Starlings first appeared in Iceland shortly before the middle of last century, first down in Hornafjörður in the southeast corner of the country, before settling in Reykjavik in the early 1960s. Despite a lot of people having little but contempt for starlings, they're among the most artistic and astute mimics of all the birds in this country, possessed of resourcefulness and excellent powers of memory. The first starlings that came to the capital apparently settled in an old wooden house on Vonarstræti Street. Living there at that time was a poet whose wife was cheerful and inclined to laughter. That was the first sound the starlings learned in their new city, and they've preserved it in their own rostral tradition ever since.

The poet has recently attested to this in a published poem that describes how his wife's laughter can still be heard here and there throughout the town, in the gardens where the starlings have made their homes.

And now, the old lumber worker told of how a great flock of starlings took up residence in the Lumberyard, some of them sheer geniuses at imitating the sound of the table saw. Time and again during lunch and coffee breaks, the workers there thought that unauthorised individuals had gotten to the saws and turned them on, so ordinary were the sounds, but it always turned out to be starlings mimicking the racket made by the handlers as they tossed boards and planks onto the stacks.

Only then did the residents turn their attention to these birds, and were greatly relieved to realise that the sounds were of this world. An exterminator was called. He showed up with an extremely noisy high-pressure sprayer and sprayed poison over the starling congregation, causing most to drop like flies in a very short time, although some did manage to fly away and escape the massacre.

A month later, the starlings had returned with a large number of reinforcements. Since then, not a moment of peace has been had in those buildings due to this murmuration of starlings, which expertly mimic the noise of the poison sprayer. The apartments there are selling slowly, if at all, and many of the considerably few residents who had already moved in have apparently begun to think about packing their things and going.

When His Eyes are on You, You're the Virgin Mary

Guðrún Eva Mínervudóttir

Translated by Meg Matich

SOME DAYS ARE WORSE than others. When I'm so lonely my blood thickens and slows to a slog in my veins. Those days, it's impossible to do anything but sit in the half-light and wait for the murmur of voices to overwhelm the static in my ears. If I can persuade myself to drink black coffee, I study my reflection in it. There, I find a pair of eyes to look into, and I feel a warmth in my belly, as if somebody has said something beautiful to me. I fumble awkwardly when the bartender hands me my change, take a chance and stroke the hands of this person I do not know. The thought of all the hands that have handled this cash lingers with me, and I leave my change on the table instead of shoving it into my pocket. And all of a sudden, he's sitting beside me. Stronger than me, with kind eyes, the deep brown of coffee. He lights a cigarette, but doesn't say a word. When I feel the heat of him next to me, I turn my head. He smiles.

'Finally,' he says.

'What?' I ask.

'Finally, I got you.'

I've seen him before – often. Reykjavik is the kind of place where you encounter the same people over and over.

'You live on Laugavegur. I saw you unlock the door to a flat there once.'

'I know.'

'What do you know?'

'I know I live on Laugavegur.'

He snuffs out his cigarette with deep concentration, then picks up the filter to stub out the glowing ashes, but stops himself, drops the butt, and watches the last embers burn themselves out.

'You're just what I expected,' he says, finally turning away from the ashtray to make eye contact.

I'm not whatever he thinks I am, but I give him a Mona Lisa smile to appease him.

'I've read about how people carry themselves, and I've studied your demeanour. So when you said earlier that you know you live on Laugavegur, you only confirmed I was right.'

'I met someone once who claimed he could interpret birthmarks,' I answer.

The laughter he lets loose is more of an exclamation: Hah! Then, instantly serious again.

'Scoff at me all you like. You know how good you are at it,' he says. 'But hear me out! You live alone, or rather, alone with a tabby cat. You study sociology or philosophy at the university – you're a real bookworm – and you love Hallgrimskirkja and Hotel Borg, and the ducks in Tjörnin pond. A Reykjavik-romantic of the worst kind; that's you. You started to fledge as soon as you were on your own – and how you struggled, impatient in a seductive world. And? Life burned in your loins, but you went in circles? Oh, you bet I know you, kid. Lustful, impetuous child…'

I cut off his rant, but my voice doesn't sound like my voice:

'I don't own a cat.'

'No, but you have a special friend, who is incalculably broken and incalculably alive. He's twenty years older than you and comes and goes as he pleases. Like a tabby cat. You fuck sometimes. You practice BDSM.'

'BDSM?' I echo.

'Yes, or something like that. Here's what I think: your kink isn't wearing a dog collar. But you like to submit to him because you're innocent and pure like a little girl. He doles out little dollops of love and then breaks you down with cruel words, but he always comforts you after. But, deep down, you know he only has you and nobody but you. And he loves and tortures you in equal measure. Sometimes he cries when he orgasms, and then he forces himself to say: "Why…?" or: "I'll kill you!" or: "You you you." Words that would otherwise be left unsaid.

'And in the morning, you make him coffee, and if he tells you to do it naked, you do as he says, and he watches your every movement with the purgatorial fires of purification in his eyes and you… you are, in his eyes, purer and more unblemished than anything else, and you know that, and you live up to the name. Naked to brew coffee. When his eyes are on you, you're the Virgin Mary.'

My heart is beating out of my chest, but I can't summon a single word. He shrugs his shoulders and lights another cigarette.

'That's just how it is,' he says. 'Otherwise, you're generally satisfied. Except!' He knits his brow and points his finger in the air. 'It's as if some days are still worse than others. Days when your blood thickens and slows to a slog in your veins. You long so much to be touched that almost anyone can tempt you.'

He reaches out his hand as if I'm an animal, and he's inviting me to rub myself against his palm… And he strokes my cheek – only for a second. I jump, and before I know it, I'm standing up, staring down at him. Finding it difficult to swallow, certain that shock shows on my face. He stares disinterestedly at the table, his shoulders and back relaxed.

He looks like he hasn't spoken in a while. Lights another cigarette and smokes it slow and easy. Then I notice the door to the loo is half-open, its light spilling onto the floor. Light at the end of the tunnel. Instinct drives me towards it, into the harsh fluorescence of an exposed bulb. I collide with a woman standing in front of the mirror with a compact in one hand and a sponge in the other. Before I can apologise, the woman turns to me: 'Do what you need to do. I won't bother you,' she says in that melodious voice buxom woman seem to have at their command.

She closes and locks the door. I don't know which foot to put forward. I don't know why I'm here. She's immersed in wiping down the sponge, which fell in the sink when I barged in. I sit on the toilet and squeeze out a few drops for good measure.

'Are you throwing in the towel, my dear?' she asks. 'I was watching you two before. You and this handsome man. You've got a handle on this. I was so clumsy when I was your age.'

'What do you mean?'

'You flash that beautiful smile, promising everybody something and nobody anything. You know exactly when you should look down and when you should look back up – a bold move. But I see that I don't need to warn you. You already know what game you're playing.'

I shake my head. 'I didn't mean anything by it. It's harmless.'

I inch my way towards the door. But she's put her weight into blocking the exit. She throws back her head, laughs from her gut.

'Harmless! Never!' she chokes between waves of laughter. 'If you believe that, you'll end up with your throat slit in a ditch,' she says, a disturbing smile crossing her face.

'Okay…' I say. She smiles.

'Can I go?'

She pauses. Then says: 'It wouldn't exactly be a work of

charity to let you pass, pussy cat. I'd drown you here in the toilet if I had the courage.'

She moves just far enough to the side for me to squeeze past her.

'Get the hell out of here then, and play your dirty games,' she hisses as I slip out the door.

I sit back down beside the man. He raises his eyebrows and I notice that the crow's feet at his temples radiate outwards, like they do on the faces of happy people.

'Well?' he says.

I shrug and run the tip of my finger along the bottom of my cup, stirring the mire of sugar.

The Dead are Here With Us at Christmas

Ágúst Borgþór Sverrisson

Translated by Lytton Smith

IT WAS LATE on 24 December when we headed out to the graveyard. My mother had been at work and not returned home until the day was almost done. While Mum took me along with her, my older siblings were to start getting the house ready and preparing dinner. Outside it was sleeting but it still felt Christmassy. Snowflakes drifted past the car windows and the white blanket covering the streets lit up the darkness.

Soon after we set off, the car started to judder and for a while, my mother didn't attempt anything above 40kph. Then it seemed fine again. But the episode had made me anxious. I told her I thought we should give the graveyard a miss this Christmas. What if the car dies and we can't get back home? Mum said we were going and that was that. 'There must and will be a lit candle on your brother's grave this Christmas. There's nothing for it but to press on.'

The traffic was light; the Christmas rush was over. Yesterday, my mother had taken me in the car to buy the Christmas dinner and there had been a long train of cars along the dual carriageways, Hringbraut and Miklubraut. Now there was just an occasional car here and there. A calm lay over everything. We were late.

The car started making alarming noises again as it pulled closer to the graveyard. By the time we got to the gate, the clock showed almost quarter to six. This irritated me. I wanted to eat Christmas dinner like everyone else in Iceland: six o'clock, same as every year.

No one was walking through the grounds. Usually, it was quite busy on 24 December when we came here but this time we were really late. Far too late.

We walked into the graveyard. My brother's plot was not far from the car park and church; we went downhill a little way, then turned right onto a path until we came to the familiar, white headstone. In the dark, it was an indistinct shape but my mother had a torch; when she shone it on the stone, it illuminated a photograph of my brother, blond-haired, plump-cheeked. He had been dead three and a half years. There'd been a time when he was with us for Christmas, looking exactly like this.

Mum took a round memorial candle from a plastic bag and set it down by the headstone. She asked if I wanted to shield the flame or light the match. I chose the latter. She handed me the She handed me the box of windproof matches, crouched down over the candle, and covered it with her hands. I lit a match. The sulphurous head was green but not dark like normal matches. It smelled different. Matches always reminded me of New Year's Eve, of stars and fireworks. They always excited me, but right now I was simply frustrated at being in this irksome cemetery past six o'clock.

I bent down and guided the flame towards the candle. Its wick was many times thicker than a regular candle's. The flame lit up my mother's hands. They seemed old and weary to me, a teenager. But she wasn't old; she was 45.

The candle burned brightly and the wind hardly swayed it. The snow had stopped. White, thin as flour, it stretched along the incline until it merged into the darkness. Everything was quiet, holiday solemn, mournful, no one around but the two of us, who were meant to be heading home.

We left the graveyard, walked back to the car park and got into the car. I looked at two nearby houses. They were set apart from the rest of the residential area, almost standing inside the cemetery. All their windows were illuminated, their Christmas decorations lit. Through the living room window in one of the houses, I could see people sitting down to dinner. When we got home, everything would be ready and we would do the same. I was looking forward to it.

The car wouldn't start. Mum tried to crank the ignition again and again, persisting until the electricity was entirely spent and there was a miserable click instead of the purr of the ignition. I was used to sitting in old cars that had trouble starting. My earliest memory of that was with Dad, before he left us, back when I was little, and he cursed and yelled as he tried to start our old banger. And now, all of a sudden, it had happened to us: Christmas was here and we were stuck at the cemetery in Fossvogur. All thanks to my mother's stubbornness, and how set in her ways she was. The mobile phone had not been invented yet: this all happened back in 1975.

At first, despair overwhelmed me, then frustration began to boil over. My mother acted like she always did, taking everything in her stride. Mum never showed any sign of weakness.

'Go over to one of those houses and ask if you can make a phone call. I'm going to check the starter,' she said, as if nothing were more natural. She simply got out of the car and opened the bonnet. I knew she had no idea what to do next, it was all a show. She did not want to go to the houses herself, she did not like asking for help. She told me to call home and talk to my older brother and ask him to get hold of a man with a tow rope.

'For god's sake, why did we have to come to this stupid graveyard? You knew the car was on its last legs!' I cursed and whined.

Mum repeated her order and said it was not a big deal for people to let us borrow their phone.

The thought of knocking on a stranger's door at such a time was terrifying. But it would be even worse spending 24 December in the car park. I had no choice, so I dragged myself with heavy steps to one of the houses and rang the bell. Some time passed and then the door opened. A stocky man in his forties, wearing a white shirt and a knitted sweater, stood blocking the threshold. He looked at me in astonishment.

'Our car has broken down. Can I borrow your phone?'

'What? We're sitting down to dinner,' the man replied, looking as if all he wanted was to close the door again.

My anger towards my mother intensified. What could be more embarrassing than hassling strangers who were trying to sit down to their Christmas roast?

I pulled myself together enough to say, 'Okay, but we just need to make one phone call so someone can come get us.'

The man still hesitated there in the doorway. A female voice from inside the house asked what was going on.

'Some kid asking to use our phone,' he replied, sheepishly.

'Come now, let him in,' said the woman.

The man stood aside from the doorway but didn't explicitly invite me in. I stepped hesitantly into the hall. There were people carrying things through to the dining room table while others were already seated. No one paid any attention to me. How weird it was, being in a strange home on Christmas. I found the phone without being directed to it and I called my older brother. I resolved to never forgive my mother.

★

While we waited, my mother lit a cigarette; she did not smoke much, maybe two cigarettes a day, often sitting alone in the kitchen with the lights off. She enjoyed smoking alone in the dark. Maybe she was thinking of solutions to all the problems she struggled with, the problems she never let us know she fretted over.

A long-standing jealousy towards my little brother erupted within me. He'd gotten all the attention, being sick all the time. He'd been bought more expensive toys than me as compensation for his illness and for having to spend hour upon hour at the hospital. My mother's life had seemed to revolve around him, and only him.

I was mad and I groused about it. It was a terrible idea to have headed to the cemetery in a broken car, the trip could have waited. 'I refuse to believe you wanted your brother's grave to be the only one that was not lit up for Christmas,' she replied. I did not answer. A candlelit grave meant nothing to me. I told her she was ruining my Christmas. 'What nonsense,' she said, though she did not get angry at my wittering on. She pretended it did not affect her, that it was a trivial thing.

After we had been waiting about half an hour, a taciturn fellow in a pickup truck arrived. He was an acquaintance or co-worker of my brother's.

'Hello, Pálmi,' my mother said. 'Go on and hook us up. And remember to drive carefully.' Mum made it sound like she was directing a subordinate, not someone who was rescuing us from an embarrassing emergency.

The tow truck hauled us along the more-or-less empty city streets. Mum and I were silent. Just before we got to the house, she looked me in the eye. It's remarkable how much you can see when you look outside yourself for a moment: her face swirled with emotions: fear, guilt, imploring. In a split second, her appearance revealed all the anguish that was wrapped up within her customary assurance, her determination, her self-control.

It was half-past seven when we got home. Nothing had gone wrong after all, it was just an adjustment, we were merely going to eat Christmas dinner a little late, that was all there was to it. The food was ready and on the table, and there were Christmas presents under the tree. I, however, was still in a bad mood after the car problems and the argument.

I got into the Christmas spirit once we started eating. Not because of the food, even though it was delicious. It just happened in an instant when I looked at my younger brother's plate there at the end of the table. We always set a place for him at Christmas: a plate, cutlery, a glass and a napkin, just like the rest of us, because that's how my mother wanted it, feeling him with us in his own way. She often said she felt his presence, especially at Christmas.

My eyes lingered on his plate and suddenly a pleasant current coursed through my body. A warmth. I looked out the window to see it was snowing again. The snow swallowed down into the evening stillness, slow, soft, and ceremonious.

Many years later, now older and wiser, I can feel strong tugs of remorse at having added to my mother's worries that night, added to that suppressed anguish she'd always kept secret from us. I came to realise she'd needed to go to the graveyard and light a candle on his grave. But I was also able to forgive myself, to understand I could no more have behaved differently back then than she could.

About the Editors

Vera Júlíusdóttir is a translator and filmmaker. Her translations of Icelandic short stories have appeared in *Elsewhere: Stories from Small Town Europe* (2007) and *Decapolis: Tales from Ten Cities* (2006), both published by Comma Press. Júlíusdóttir has lived in Minneapolis and London, and now lives and works in Reykjavik.

Becca Parkinson is Engagement Manager at Comma Press and Editor of *The Book of Tbilisi* and *The Book of Riga*. She has previously served as Secretary then Chair of the Society of Young Publishers North branch (2017-2019) and was longlisted for the London Book Fair Trailblazer Award in both 2019 and 2020. She took part in the first British Council International Publishing Fellowship (2019-2020) and was appointed as Trustee of Manchester Literature Festival in 2021.

About the Authors

Guðrún Eva Mínervudóttir (b. 1976) was born in Reykjavik and spent her childhood partly in the city, partly in various villages around the country. In her youth, she was a cow-herd, sheep-minder and bartender. After publishing her first book in 1998 (*When His Eyes are on You, You're the Virgin Mary*), she became a full-time writer, and has now written and published nine novels and two collections of short stories. Since 2010, she has taught creative writing at the Iceland Academy of the Arts. Her work has been translated into several languages and has won various awards, including The National Prize for Literature in 2011 for *Everything With a Kiss Awakens*, The Icelandic Literature Prize for Women for *Love, Texas* in 2018 and the National Radio Lifetime Award for Literature in 2019. She now lives in the small town of Hveragerdi with husband Marteinn and daughter Minerva.

Ágúst Borgþór Sverrisson (b. 1962) has published six volumes of short stories and three novels, mostly set in Reykjavik. He works as a reporter and news director of DV, one of Iceland's main media outlets, and writes fiction in his spare time. His latest book is the short story collection *Afleiðingar* (*Consequences*), published in 2017.

Björn Halldórsson (b. 1983) was born in Reykjavik. He studied English and American Literature at the University of East-Anglia in Norwich, and has an MFA in Creative Writing from the University of Glasgow. His short stories have been published by literary journals in Iceland and the UK and have also appeared in translation in German, Italian and Hebrew. His first book, a short story collection titled *Smáglæpir* (*Misdemeanours*), was published in 2017, and his second book, *Stol* (*Route 1*), a novel, was published in early 2021. He lives in Reykjavik with his wife.

Friðgeir Einarsson is an Icelandic writer and theatre-artist. His published work includes two collections of short stories, *Takk fyrir að láta mig vita* (*Thank you for letting me know*, 2016) and *Ég hef séð svona áður* (*I've Seen This Before*, 2018), and the novel *Formaður húsfélagsins* (*Chairman of the Homeowner's Association*, 2017). His play *Club Romantica* was awarded the Icelandic Theatre Awards in 2019 for Best Play.

Andri Snær Magnason (b. 1973) has won the Icelandic Literary Prize in every category; fiction, children's fiction and non-fiction. Magnason also writes poetry, plays, short stories and essays. He has been awarded the French Grand Prix de l'Imaginaire, the West Nordic Literature Prize and The Kairos Prize. In 2009, he co-directed the documentary *Dreamland*, which was based on his book *Dreamland: A Self-Help Manual for a Frightened Nation*. His most recent work, *On Time and Water*, was nominated for the Nordic Council Literature Prize 2021. His books have been translated into almost 40 languages. Magnason ran for president of Iceland in 2016 and came third out of nine candidates.

Auður Jónsdóttir (b. 1973) is a writer and freelance journalist. She writes novels, short stories, non-fiction and books for children and teenagers, among them a book about her grandfather, the Nobel laureate Halldór Laxness. Jónsdóttir has won the Icelandic Literary Prize, the Icelandic Women's Literature Prize and twice been nominated for the Nordic Council Literature Prize. Her books have been translated into eight languages and several films have been made based on her novels.

Einar Már Guðmundsson (b. 1954) is a novelist, short story writer, poet, screenwriter and translator. He has received many awards and distinctions for his books, in Iceland and abroad, such as the Icelandic Literary Prize, Nordic Council Literature Prize, Norwegian Bjørnson Prize, the Scharnberg Memorial Award in Denmark, The Karen Blixen Medal, and The Giuseppe Acerbi Literary Prize in Italy. In 2012, he received the Nordic Council Literature Prize, for his contribution to literature. Guðmundsson's works have been translated into more than 30 languages and a film based on his novel *Angels of the Universe* featured music from Icelandic band Sigur Rós.

Fríða Ísberg (b. 1992) is an Icelandic author and poet based in Reykjavik. Her short story collection, *Itch*, was nominated for the Nordic Council Literature Prize in 2020, as well as the Icelandic Women's Literature Prize and won The Icelandic Booksellers' Prize. Her work has been translated into five languages and has appeared in various publications abroad as well as at home. She occasionally writes reviews for *The Times Literary Supplement*. Ísberg is also a member of the poetry collective Impostor Poets and has published three books of poetry with the collective.

Kristín Eiríksdóttir (b. 1981) is an award-winning novelist, short story writer, translator, poet, and playwright. Her novel *A Fist or a Heart* was nominated for the Nordic Council Literature Prize and won the Icelandic Literary Prize as well as the Icelandic Women's Literature Prize. The book was selected as one of the 2019 Best World Literature, by *Library Journal* and her short fiction has appeared in *Best European Fiction 2011*. Her work has been translated into six languages. Alongside writing, Eiríksdóttir is a visual artist and has participated in group exhibitions and shows. She frequently merges visual art and poetry in her works.

Þórarinn Eldjárn (b. 1949) has published numerous collections of poetry and children's verse, short story collections and novels and translated fiction for adults and children, including works by Strindberg, Göran Tunström and Lewis Carroll as well as Shakespere's *King Lear, Macbeth, A Midsummer Night's Dream* and *Hamlet* for the Icelandic National Theatre. Eldjarn is the recipient of many awards. His novel *The Blue Tower* was shortlisted for the Aristeion – the European literature and translation prize, nominated for the Nordic Council Literature Prize and for the IMPAC Dublin Award. His work has been translated into fourteen languages and two of his novels have been adapted to screen.

About the Translators

Philip Roughton is an award-winning translator of Icelandic literature. He earned a PhD in Comparative Literature from the University of Colorado, Boulder, with specialties in medieval Icelandic, medieval Chinese, and Latin literature, and wrote his dissertation on medieval Icelandic translations of saints' and apostles' lives. He has taught modern and world literature at CU-Boulder, and medieval literature at the University of Iceland. His translations include works by Halldór Laxness, Jón Kalman Stefánsson, Steinunn Sigurðardóttir, and others.

Victoria Cribb spent a number of years travelling, studying and working in Iceland before becoming a full-time translator in 2002. She has translated more than thirty books by Icelandic authors, including Andri Snær Magnason, Arnaldur Indriðason, Gyrðir Elíasson, Ragnar Jónasson, Sjón and Yrsa Sigurðardóttir. A number of these works have been nominated for prizes, most recently *CoDex 1962* by Sjón, long-listed for the 2019 Best Translated Book Award (Fiction) and the PEN America Translation Prize. In 2017, she received the Orðstír honorary translation award for services to Icelandic literature

Larissa Kyzer is a writer and Icelandic literary translator. Her translation of Kristín Eiríksdóttir's *A Fist or a Heart* was awarded the American Scandinavian Foundation's 2019 translation prize. The same year, she was one of Princeton University's Translators in Residence. In 2020, Larissa cofounded Eth & Thorn, a chapbook press dedicated to Icelandic poetry and short fiction in translation. She is co-chair of PEN America's Translation Committee and runs the virtual Women+ in Translation reading series Jill!

Meg Matich has received support for her literary translation work from PEN, Fulbright, the Icelandic Literature Center , and others, and frequently collaborates with UNESCO Reykjavik. She received the PEN/Heim for her translation of Magnús Sigurðsson's *Cold Moons* (Phoneme Media, 2017), which composer David R. Scott subsequently translated into a choral symphony. In 2018, Meg translated an anthology in honour of the world's first democratically elected woman president, Vigdís Finnbogadóttir (2019) and collaborated with Sigurðsson on an Icelandic poetry edition of *The Cafe Review*. Her translation of Þóra Hjörleifsdóttir's *Magma* is forthcoming from Grove Atlantic (US) and Picador (UK), and her translation of Auður Jónsdóttir's *Quake* is forthcoming from Dottir Press. She is the former director of The Poetry Brothel Reykajvik and producer of the forthcoming immersive performance *The Poetry Apothecary* (*Ljóðatek*). Her translations have appeared in or are forthcoming from *PEN America, Exchanges, Words Without Borders, Asymptote, Gulf Coast,* and others.

Lytton Smith is the translator of over a dozen novels and non-fiction works from the Icelandic, including, most recently, Andri Snær Magnason's *On Time and Water* (Serpent's Tail, 2020). His translations of *Tómas Jónsson, Bestseller* by Guðbergur Bergsson (Open Letter) and *Öræfi* by Ófeigur sigurðsson (Deep Vellum) were finalists for the Best Translated Book Award in the United States in 2018 and 2019 respectively. He is a 2019 National Endowment for the Arts Literature Translation Fellowship recipient. His most recent poetry collection, *The Square,* was published by New Michigan Press in March 2021. He lives in western upstate New York where he teaches creative writing, Black Studies, and literature at SUNY Geneseo and serves as the Director of the Center for Integrative Learning.

Special Thanks

The editors would like to thank Valgerður Benediktsdóttir, Alda Björk Valdimarsdóttir and Sigríður Pétursdóttir for their help.

READING THE CITY SERIES

The Book of Birmingham • Edited by Khavita Bhanot

The Book of Cairo • Edited by Raph Cormack

The Book of Dhaka • Edited by Arunava Sinha
& Pushpita Alam

The Book of Gaza • Edited by Atef Abu Saif

The Book of Havana • Edited by Orsola Casagrande

The Book of Tehran • Edited by Fereshteh Ahmadi

The Book of Istanbul • Edited by Jim Hinks & Gul Turner

The Book of Jakarta • Edited by Maesy Ang
& Teddy W. Kusuma

The Book of Khartoum • Edited by Raph Cormack
& Max Shmookler

The Book of Leeds • Edited by Tom Palmer & Maria Crossan

The Book of Liverpool • Edited by Maria Crossan & Eleanor
Rees

The Book of Newcastle • Edited by Angela Readman & Zoe
Turner

The Book of Riga • Edited by Becca Parkinson & Eva Eglaja-
Kristsone

The Book of Rio • Edited by Toni Marques & Katie Slade

The Book of Shanghai • Edited by Dai Congrong & Jin Li

The Book of Sheffield • Edited by Catherine Taylor

The Book of Tbilisi • Edited by Becca Parkinson
& Gvantsa Jobava

The Book of Tokyo • Edited by Jim Hinks, Masashi Matsuie
& Michael Emmerich

The Book of Venice • Edited by Orsola Casagrande

The Book of Venice

Edited by Orsola Casagrande

The Venice presented in these stories is a far cry from the 'impossibly beautiful', frozen-in-time city so familiar to the thousands who flock there every year – a city about which, Henry James once wrote, 'there is nothing new to be said.' Instead, they represent the other Venice, the one tourists rarely see: the real, everyday city that Venetians have to live and work in.

Rather than a city in stasis, we see it at a crossroads, fighting to regain its radical, working-class soul, regretting the policies that have seen it turn slowly into a theme park, and taking the pandemic as an opportunity to rethink what kind of city it wants to be.

Featuring: Elisabetta Baldisserotto, Gianfranco Bettin, Annalisa Bruni, Michele Catozzi, Cristiano Dorigo, Roberto Ferrucci, Ginevra Lamberti, Samantha Lenarda, Marilia Mazzeo & Enrico Palandri

ISBN: 978-1-91097-409-4
£9.99

The Book of Jakarta

Edited by Maesy Ang & Teddy W. Kusuma

Made up of over 17,000 islands, Indonesia is the fourth most populous country on the planet. It is home to hundreds of different ethnicities and languages, and a cultural identity that is therefore constantly in flux. Like the country as a whole, the capital Jakarta is a multiplicity of irreducible, unpredictable and contradictory perspectives.

From down-and-out philosophers to roadside entertainers, the characters in these stories see Jakarta from all angles. Traversing different neighbourhoods and social strata, their stories capture the energy, aspirations, and ever-changing landscape of what is also the world's fastest-sinking city.

Featuring: utiuts, Sabda Armandio, Hanna Fransisca, Cyntha Hariadi, Afrizal Malna, Dewi Kharisma Michellia, Ratri Ninditya, Yusi Avianto Pareanom, Ben Sohib & Ziggy Zezsyazeoviennazabrizkie

ISBN: 978-1-91269-732-8
£9.99

The Book of Shanghai

Edited by Dai Congrong & Jin Li

The characters in this literary exploration of one of the world's biggest cities are all on a mission. Whether it is responding to events around them, or following some impulse of their own, they are defined by their determination – a refusal to lose themselves in a city that might otherwise leave them anonymous, disconnected, alone.

From the neglected mother whose side-hustle in collecting sellable waste becomes an obsession, to the schoolboy determined to end a long-standing feud between his family and another, these characters show a defiance that reminds us why Shanghai – despite its hurtling economic growth –remains an epicentre for individual creativity.

Featuring: Wang Anyi, Xiao Bai, Shen Dacheng, Chen Danyan, Cai Jun, Chen Qiufan, Xia Shang, Teng Xiaolan, Fu Yuehui & Wang Zhanhei

ISBN: 978-1-91269-727-4
£9.99